ALL WORKS BY BENJAMIN WALLACE

DUCK & COVER ADVENTURES
Post-Apocalyptic Nomadic Warriors (A Duck & Cover Adventure Book 1)
Knights of the Apocalypse (A Duck & Cover Adventure Book 2)
Pursuit of the Apocalypse (A Duck & Cover Adventure Book 3)
Tales of the Apocalypse (Volume 1) – Summer 2016

BULLETPROOF ADVENTURES OF DAMIAN STOCKWELL
Horror in Honduras (The Bulletproof Adventures of Damian Stockwell)
Terrors of Tesla (The Bulletproof Adventures of Damian Stockwell)
The Mechanical Menace (The Bulletproof Adventures of Damian Stockwell)

DAD VERSUS
Dad Versus The Grocery Store
Dads Versus The World (Volume 1)
Dads Versus Zombies

OTHER BOOKS
Tortugas Rising
Junkers

UNCIVIL
UnCivil: The Immortal Engine
UnCivil: Vanderbilt's Behemoth

SHORT STORIES
Alternate Realty
Dystopia Inc. #1: The War Room
Pilgrim (A Short Story)

Visit benjaminwallacebooks.com for more info.

BENJAMIN WALLACE

Copyright © 2016 by Benjamin Wallace.
All rights reserved.

ISBN-13: 978-1533632319
ISBN-10: 1533632316

This is a work of fiction. Names, characters, places, and incidents are the product of the author's imagination. Any resemblance to actual persons, living or dead, events, or locales is entirely coincidental.

Cover design by J Caleb Designs.
www.jcalebdesign.com

PRELUDE

He hated walking. It went against everything he believed in. Physical exertion of any kind wasn't really his thing at all. He was completely against manual labor. It's why he became a farmer in the first place.

No lifting. No sweating. It was the farmer's life for him. All you had to do was sit back and watch the drones work.

On a bad day you might have to take the controls and pilot the drone yourself. That was about as bad as it got. He'd heard stories of some farmers having to go into the field to check on malfunctioning equipment, but until now, he'd never really believed it. He figured they were stories farmers passed around to scare off the masses from such a cushy job.

That's why, when the alarm first came up, he assumed it was the day shift pulling a prank on him. Those guys had a hard time telling the difference between being funny and being dicks. Even at that, this wasn't their best work.

A few keystrokes sent the drones to investigate and he kicked back to plot his revenge. The day shift foolishly left their food unguarded in the communal fridge overnight, and spiking their drink with some Nanolax would be a good start to the retaliation. He figured they could laugh at him all they wanted as long as a million microbots kept them glued to a toilet.

A chirp indicated that the drone had arrived at the site of the alarm and found nothing. Nothing at all. The equipment that was sending the alarm wasn't even there. He set a search path and the drones began running the preset pattern.

He kicked back in his chair, much to the dismay of its springs, and put his feet up on the console.

Watching the cornstalks zoom past the fish-eyed lens had made him queasy. Every row was the same. Every stalk was identical. Every leaf and ear was pitched at the same angle. They had been designed that way to ensure maximum exposure to the sun, but the whole effect worked to lull him into a trance.

He spent an hour searching the cornfield for the missing machinery to no avail and was on the verge of passing out when a series of damaged stalks broke the monotony and provided the first clue as to what was happening. Seizing the controls, he piloted the drone back down the row then turned to follow the broken plants.

Something had crashed through the crop. Someone was making off with the equipment.

He sat forward in his chair and willed the drone to follow the trail. He smiled. This was no longer work, it was crime fighting. Capturing the thief on the camera was all it would take for the authorities to identify the culprits. But he would be the hero, and for the second time in his life he might even trend. He smiled at the thought of this story supplanting the old one in the feeds. Finally.

"'Never live it down' my ass," he muttered to himself as he pushed harder on the control pad.

Sweeping through the crops, he followed the busted stalks and fallen ears of corn. He wasn't a farmer anymore. He was a fighter jockey piloting the latest generation WarBird through enemy canyons. The whir of the rotors played through his monitor's speakers, but they weren't quite fitting to the mood so he made his own scramjet engine sounds until he reached the center of the cornfield and stopped the drone.

There it was. A shadow moving quickly between the plants. Each time the figure darted, another plant fell to the ground with the dry crack of firewood.

He chased after the shadow for two rows and turned right to follow. But there was nothing there. The trail of destruction had ended. He flipped the drone 180 degrees in a deft move he would have to recount to the reporters later.

For a brief instant, the figure filled the monitor. Then everything went dead.

The drone dropped from the air and landed with its camera pointed toward the night sky.

Corn swayed in and out of view through a cracked lens, but the machine no longer responded to his touch. He could hear nothing but the breeze.

"No!" he screamed as the headlines faded from his daydreams. He shot up with such speed that his chair sailed back across the room, spinning as it went. He didn't wait for it to stop. He pulled a denim coat from a hook by the door with one hand and a shotgun with the other as he dashed out the door into the night. He had to bring these evildoers to justice. He had to have another fifteen minutes—a better fifteen minutes—of fame. They could take whatever busted piece of farm equipment they wanted from the company, but they couldn't take that opportunity away from him.

The utility vehicle whirred into action. Knobby off-road tires skipped on the concrete before biting into the dirt with an unbreakable hold and catapulting him into the cornfield. A thousand acres separated him from his prey, but he wasn't going to let it get away. He kept the pedal to the floor.

The cart's suspension ate the uneven soil without complaint and kicked the looser earth into the air behind it as it went.

Much like the view through the drone, the rows of corn blended into a mesh of green silk as he zipped past. This time he accepted it. He kept his eyes forward and let his peripheral look for the trail. The broken stalks would be a sore thumb sticking out in the genetically engineered pattern.

They were. He stood on the brakes when he spotted them and turned the cart into the path. The ride grew rougher as he crossed the furrows and the cart threw him back and forth, left and right, but he pressed on and let the cart jostle him about until he found the downed drone.

The cart idled in complete silence as he stepped into the field. He was alone.

Breathing heavily from the excitement, he was startled by how loud his breath was in the middle of the night. He swallowed hard once to try to hold it back and exhaled slowly before approaching the fallen drone.

The device was peppered with holes. The rotors were shattered. Shot clean off. He bent to examine the wreckage more closely.

There was a snap and a nearby corn stalk fell.

He hurried back to the cart and grabbed the shotgun. He racked a shell into the chamber and turned back to the crop.

"Show yourself."

There was no response.

He took a cautious step away from the vehicle. "You're not supposed to be out here."

Again, there was no response. There was no sound at all.

He racked the shotgun. The unspent shell fell to the ground and he closed his eyes at his mistake. "You're trespassing. Do you know what that means?"

He bent down and grabbed the shell off the ground. "That means I can shoot you. Legally. That's what that means."

He plugged the shell back into the bottom of the gun.

"I don't want to shoot you." He so wanted to shoot them. He was terrified. But being the hero behind the trigger instead of the hero behind the camera was going to ensure him at least a half-day in the top fifty stories. Number one in the farm feeds for sure.

Another stalk cracked a few rows over and he dove into the corn. The leaves whipped at his face as he fought through the tight plantings and burst through into the furrowed earth.

He turned and saw the figure a few yards away.

The shotgun bucked in his hands as he fired from the hip. He felt the blast in his ears, then heard it, then watched sparks dance as the shot bounced harmlessly off the metal scarecrow rooted in the field.

The robot stood on spindly, telescopic legs that enabled it to set its head above the crop. Its straw hat flopped around, leaving only the lower half of its face visible.

"Good thing the news didn't see that." He chuckled to himself and fired at the lanky sentry again. "Damn thing scared me."

The scarecrow took the blast in silence.

Its eyes began to glow red.

"What are you... You're supposed to be offline at night."

The machine looked right at him. Hydraulics in the legs lowered the body into the cornfield. Then it took a step toward him.

He ran.

Against everything he stood for, he ran. He broke

through the stalks and sent them falling to the ground as he scrambled back toward the cart.

He had only made it two rows when he heard the scarecrow's Gatling gun begin to whir.

1

It was a bright cold day in September and the clock struck thirteen. Nothing in the office worked right.

Jake took out a long list entitled "Broken Shit" and added the clock to the bottom beneath everything else that needed his attention.

He scanned the list. This needed that. That needed this. This thing was making that noise. This was leaking something most likely hazardous. It went on.

The list had been shoved in and out of the drawer so many times that the paper itself was falling apart. There were more important things on the list than a broken clock, but none of it was going to get fixed without money. And to get money they needed a job.

He looked at the phone and willed it to ring. He willed at it for five minutes before giving up. He shoved the list back in the drawer, stood up and pulled the malfunctioning timepiece off the wall. He gave it one last look before tossing it in the trashcan. Even if the phone did ring and even if the job did actually pay, it's not like he was going to spend the money on a stupid clock.

Since the phone wasn't cooperating and he no longer had a clock to watch, there wasn't much reason to stay in the office. He did the books by moving the envelopes on the desk marked "FINAL NOTICE" to the trashcan and stepped into the shop to see if he could help with anything.

The first thing that hit him was the sound of work, clattering, clanging and some grunting, the crew pounding something into place somewhere in the back. It didn't sound like it was going well.

The next thing that hit him was the question of the day.

"Hey, Jake, do you think ankles are sexy?"

The man behind the question was kicked back in a chair, behind a book, with his feet up on a coffee table. His name was Mitch Pritchard, but since he was full of cybernetic parts and horrible ideas everyone on the team called him Glitch. Glitch had been big and strong before he started adding parts to himself. Now he was twice as wide as a person should be and whirred when he walked. He called these enhancements "oddmentations" because even though Glitch tried to sound smart, he really wasn't.

The ankle question rolled through Jake's head, trying to land in a place where it would make sense, but nothing stuck. "What?"

"Do you think ankles are sexy?" Glitch pulled up his pant leg and pointed at his own ankle like he was presenting Exhibit A.

Jake put his hands up between himself and the ankle. "I'd really rather you leave me out of your upgrades, Glitch."

The big man laughed and leaned forward. He held up the book and tried to explain himself. "I'm reading this book about the court of King Charles Vee Eye Eye and there was this woman named Agnes Sorel that started a fashion trend. She'd show up with her boobs all hanging out. That would be the modern equivalent of walking into the White House with your nipples saluting the President."

"Glitch..." he tried to interrupt, but he had lost the manmachine to either a vivid imagined scene or a hardly safe-for-work reference image on his optic implant.

"And then other women started doing it, too. They wore dresses with their boobs all hanging out. BUT, they always had their ankles covered because it was considered scandalous to show ankles. And I thought, I never thought the ankle was really hot, but I don't know, maybe I've just seen too many, you know? Like I've been overexposed to ankles and I became desensitized to their inherent sexiness. And then I thought, maybe we're really missing out on this ankle thing." His eyes wandered to a wall and a smile grew across his face. There was no telling what he was seeing.

"Glitch..."

The cyborg's attention snapped back to Jake. "Well what do you think?"

"I think, for the first time ever, reading has made someone dumber."

"Says you. But I could be onto something big with this ankle thing. It could be a big market." He leaned back in the chair and returned to his reading.

Jake shook his head, hoping any memory of the conversation would refuse to stick. Thankfully the thought was replaced by another. "Hey, Glitch?"

"Yeah, boss."

"What's everyone up to?"

"I don't know. Working or something."

"Do you think maybe you should help?"

"Nah." He pointed to a mechanical joint that served as his elbow. "You see that regulator? It's been giving me fits lately. If it acts up while I'm helping out, I hate to think of the damage it could do. I could kill somebody. But don't worry. I'm going to get it fixed."

"Yeah? And when is that?"

He shrugged and turned the page. "I'm waiting on a part."

"Everything around here is broken." Jake muttered, and walked away, leaving Glitch to his book and his assortment of dumb ideas.

The diamond plate stairs rattled beneath his feet as he descended into the garage. There was an alternating stream of clangs and curses coming from beneath a monstrous red, white and rusted truck. A pair of legs stuck out from beneath the vehicle and kicked with every grunt and stomped with every swear word as their owner beat at something on the Beast's underbelly.

The Beast was a 1974 Travelall from International Harvester. It was seventeen feet long, just as wide, and illegal in every state. Its operation required a host of special permits, certifications, and the blessing of the local constabulary. And you had to have a really good reason for driving it.

In their line of work they needed a vehicle that was off the grid. Almost half their business, when there was business, came from shutting down gridsmart cars that had become a little too smart for their own good. And since being connected to the city's traffic system made for a pretty ineffective and extremely unexciting chase, they needed the ability to move independently of the highway systems.

The Beast weighed more than two tons before their equipment was loaded. A massive 401 cubic-inch engine made it go, while drum brakes and hope made it stop. It didn't go extremely fast, but the machinist had managed to bore, beg and coax the massive V-8 into putting out over 500 foot-pounds of torque. It would move if it had to.

More swearing found its way from the floor and up through the open hood. The voice behind the curses was soft and sweet even if it was damning the truck's mother to horribly foul acts in hell and other uncomfortable locations.

Jake gave a gentle rap on the fender. "What's the matter with her now?"

"It's an ancient piece of shit held together with nothing but my genius and your empty promises. Guess which of those is broken."

"You know I'd never blame your genius, but what's wrong?"

Casters rolled against concrete and the machinist's legs

disappeared under the truck. He heard the creeper spin and a moment later her head emerged from under the chrome bumper.

She wore coveralls and engine grease like other women wore ermine and makeup. She had fine dark hair that she refused to keep short despite the safety hazard it caused to both herself and the people around her that she distracted with it.

"This thing is older than both of us put together," she said. "That's what's wrong with it. The patches are falling off the patches I patched the patches with. I need parts."

"Parts aren't cheap, Kat."

"No, but you certainly are."

"If I had it to give I would. But you know things have been slow. We all have to make do with what we have right now. You don't hear Mason complaining, do you?"

There was a red flash, a white spark, a quick dimming of the lights and a blue streak that ended with the word *sonofabitchinlittleprick* being shouted from the back of the shop.

Kat smiled, tilted her head and disappeared back under the truck.

Jake hurried to the back of the workshop. It smelled like a thunderstorm had rolled through which, he had to admit, was more pleasant than it usually smelled.

Mason stood back from a disassembled disrupter pack and alternated between waving his hand through the air and shoving it into his mouth. The man was in mid-suck on a finger when Jake rushed up.

"Mason, are you okay? What was that?"

He jumped up and down for a moment before shoving his

hand between his thighs. Bent over, he pointed a damning finger with his free hand at the device on the workbench. "That little shit bit me."

"Is your hand okay?"

"It's fine."

"Let's look at it."

Mason stomped his foot, straightened up and let the arm hang at his side. "It's fine, Mom."

"Are you sure?"

"It's fine."

"What were you doing?"

"I'm fixing this damned disrupter. It's been shorting out."

Jake tried to spy a look at the hand, but Mason tucked it behind his back. Jake shrugged away any concern he had left and asked, "Why don't you let Savant do that?"

"Oh. That's a good idea, Jake. We'll let the technician do the technical work. I should have thought of that. You kids are so damn smart. Or maybe I'm just old and stupid."

Jake tried not to smile. Mason was only a few years older than himself, but he wore each year of difference like a decade. To him, Jake was just one of those damn kids these days. He often reminded Mason of their closeness in age but now he just nodded. "He's not here."

Mason grabbed a screwdriver from the floor and turned back to the workbench. "Of course he's not here."

"He should be. Where is he?"

Mason shrugged and shoved the screwdriver back into the backpack-sized device, aiming for a screw head Jake couldn't see.

"He's running somewhere. He's climbing something. Or he's falling off something else. Don't worry. I'm sure he'll tell us all about it when he gets back. Then he'll tell us all about it again."

"Just leave it for him."

"No. It needs to get done. If I leave it for him, it'll never happen. Besides, it's my gear so it's my ass if it doesn't work right. Savant'll be just fine back in the truck. The lazy brat."

There was a *zzzt* from inside the disrupter and Mason jumped back a step onto one leg with his forearm over his face. He held the pose for a moment and looked cautiously over his arm.

"What's wrong with it?" Jake asked.

"It's a piece of junk."

Jake sighed, preparing to explain once more how no money meant no new things. "Look, I'd get a new one but..."

"No, thank you. The new ones are even worse. Everything now is just made to break. So you have to buy a new one. Not like it was before. Now if you don't mind, I have to be careful not to shock myself again." He placed the screwdriver back in the device once more.

"Shouldn't you unhook the power before you do that?"

"Why? I'd just have to hook it back up again anyway."

Jake rolled his eyes. "Duh. Stupid me."

"Your words."

Jake turned and stepped away as the lights dimmed, the sparks flew and Mason screamed, "*Sonofabitchinlittleprick!*"

He trudged back across the shop and back up the metal stairs toward his office with numbers running through his head. All of them had minus signs in front of them.

Glitch stopped him short of the door with an upraised hand.

"I don't want to talk about ankles or 16th-century exhibitionists, Glitch. I just want to go to my office."

"Your uncle's here."

Jake looked at the office door and sighed. "I don't want to go to my office." He opened the door anyway.

Uncle Aaron was sitting behind the desk, bouncing back and forth in the chair. His grin grew larger when Jake stepped in. "There he is."

"Hey, Aaron."

"'Hey, Aaron?'" The older man stood and moved around the desk with a spring in his step that said *I need a few bucks but I'll pay you back*. He stretched out his arms. "You don't have a hug for your favorite uncle?"

Jake didn't move.

"Okay," said Uncle Aaron. "I guess it is kind of weird to hug your business partner, isn't it?"

Jake shook his head, embraced the man and grimaced as three hard smacks landed on his back.

"That's a good boy. Now I won't have to tell your mother you weren't happy to see me."

Jake worked his way around the desk and sat in his chair. He felt the spring pop a little more than usual before the seat locked in a position that wasn't comfortable. He would have to add it to the list. "What can I do for you, Aaron?"

The old man sat on the desk and leaned forward. "How's our business?"

"It sucks."

"Then sell. I'll sign whatever I need to."

"There's nothing to sell. Everything's broken." Jake jerked a thumb toward the office door. "Even Glitch."

"The money's in the name."

"Ashley's Robot Reclamation of Green Hill? Do you think?"

"Well, then make it an acronym."

"No one is going to buy ARRGH," Jake said.

"You never know until you try."

Jake Ashley's eyes narrowed on his uncle. The grin on his face was a little too big to be truly genuine, but there was something new in it. "What's her name?"

Aaron stood up and waved the question off. "I don't know what you're talking about."

"Your new girlfriend. What's her name? Skylar? Tiffany? Cinnamon?"

Uncle Aaron sat in the guest chair and smiled. "Meagan."

"Hmm," Jake said. "She doesn't sound like a former stripper at all."

"She's not."

"Then she must be crazy."

"I'll have you know she is an executive director. Does that sound crazy?"

"Depends on what she's an executive director of."

Uncle Aaron turned his chair as he answered, possibly hoping the squeak would cover his response. "Society for the Preservation of Humans."

"Society for the…"

"Yes. Yes. Society for the Preservation of Humans. So what?"

"A humans first organization? The big one, even. She sounds well balanced."

"It's just a job. Look, do you have anything for me or not?"

"Not."

"Damn it, Jake." Uncle Aaron stood and gestured toward the office door. "This place is going down. We have to get out while we can."

"You're pretty much out already."

"Then save yourself and my five percent." He slammed his palms onto the desk.

Jake let out a cough. "Three percent."

He slammed his palms on the desk again. "My three percent. It's time to end it."

"Quit?"

"Yes, quit."

"Dad always said that Ashleys aren't quitters."

"He was full of shit. Of course we're quitters. We're born quitters. I quit things all the time. C'mon, Jake, be a quitter with me." Uncle Aaron smiled his uncle's smile and sat back down. The smile faded into one of his rare serious moments. "Look, Jake. The business is dying. Not just ours, but the whole industry. They're making bots better. And even the shitty ones come with a longer warranty. Pretty soon it will be just the corporate boys junking their mistakes. There's no room for the little guy anymore."

The independent shops were closing. Or selling. Or failing. But Jake wasn't ready to give up just yet.

"I heard from a buyer, Jake."

"Who would want to buy this place?"

"It doesn't matter who they are. All that matters is that they're interested and they've got more money than a whore after the Super Bowl."

Jake leaned forward in his seat. "I'm not quitting." He stood and crossed the office.

"Be honest, Jake." Uncle Aaron stood and pointed to the phone on the desk. "When was the last time that phone rang?"

The phone rang.

Uncle Aaron dropped his arm. "Well that is just the worst timing ever."

Jake grabbed the phone. "Ashley's Robot Reclamation."

"I mean a guy is just trying to make a point and the stupid thing just rings all over it. I hate machines."

Jake held up a finger to shush his uncle and turned back to the phone. He answered the caller's question. "Yes, we're junkers."

2

The Beast was named for its size and lumbering gait in traffic. But that didn't mean it didn't sound like a beast, too. The engine roared. The brakes shrieked. And there was a growl from a source that Kat had never been able to quite pin down.

The sixty-year-old vehicle charged through traffic like an elephant with hurt feelings, trumpeting over the quiet hum generated by the electric cars that filled the road.

By law, passenger cars had to be aware of their surroundings, and a hundred sensors in each vehicle were screaming at their guidance systems to get out of the way of the big red truck as it barreled through town. Traffic parted before the team as the Travelall bullied its way to the edge of the city and into the night.

They lined the bench seats and did their best not to bounce against each other as the Beast swayed back and forth on exhausted shocks. The interior smelled of fuel and exhaust and the odor mixed with the unending motion turned Jake's stomach. He fought the queasy sensation and focused on what lay ahead.

He made sure he knew where the window crank was and said, "Tell us what we're looking at, Mason."

"Okay." Mason produced a tablet and began to read the information. "Two hours ago some fat farmer walked into his cornfield and…"

"Mason." Jake interrupted and instantly recalled a dozen conversations that had started this way.

"What?"

"Forget the commentary. Just give us the facts."

"It is a fact, Jake. The dude weighed like three hundy."

"It's irrelevant. And rude."

"Well, I'm sorry, Miss Manners, but I think it is relevant to know that the bot we're looking for took down something the size of a buffalo with no trouble. Now, if it was me going in there, and it is by the way, I think that's something I'd want to know."

Jake gave a reluctant nod and looked out the window.

"This is about safety, Jake. And, honestly, I'm a little hurt that you'd think this was about anything other than the wellbeing of my coworkers."

Jake waved him back toward the tablet. "Just get on with it."

"No." Mason set the tablet in his lap. "I'd like an apology

first."

"Are you serious?"

"Are you sorry?"

Jake rolled his eyes. "Fine. I'm sorry I accused you of being insensitive."

"That's more like it." Mason lifted the tablet once more. "As I was saying, this fatty in the dell here waddles into his corn crop about two hours ago, possibly to check on a malfunctioning piece of equipment or, more likely, to make a sandwich."

Jake pounded the door. "Mason!"

"They found him dead with corn embedded in his chest," he read. "Oh big surprise, food killed him."

Jake pinched the bridge of his nose. It didn't help the growing headache as much as he'd hoped. "Just tell us what we're up against."

"It's a ZUMR, Model number R34-P3R Organic Compliant Deterrent System." He held up the screen to show everyone a blue-line schematic of the machine.

"It looks like a scarecrow," Glitch said.

"Points for you, Tin Man. That's exactly what it is." Mason turned the tablet back so he could read more. "Here's an ad for it. It suggests putting a hat and shirt on the thing for that old farm feel. Gives everyone a touch of the nostalgies I guess. But underneath the stupid hat it's a state-of-the-art murder murderer. You can tell from the oh so clever headline, 'Scares Crows Dead.'" He read further ahead to himself. "That's weird. The thing's brand new."

"It does what to crows?" Glitch asked. "How does it do that?"

"It fires corn kernels at about 2500 feet per second from this mini-gun on its right arm. And cuts them up with the scythe-looking thing on its left." He held the screen toward Glitch and waited for the cyborg to process the image.

"That's a terrible idea!"

"It's quite genius, actually. I can't imagine corn makes a very good bullet. So, what better way to make up for accuracy than with an insane amount of volume?"

"That's not what I meant and you know it. I mean, how can they get away with killing the birds?"

Mason shrugged. "It's a part of ZUMR's guilt-free farming line. The corn is all natural. So is crow blood. Crow feathers. Crow guts, too. So the crops remain completely organic, legal, and free of flying vermin." Mason paused and chuckled. "Scares crows dead. I get it now."

"You think this is funny?" Kat asked from behind the wheel.

"Pretty funny. Yeah."

"You're a horrible person, Mason," Kat said.

Mason shrugged again. "Okay."

Jake turned back from the window and glared at Mason. "Enough! Just tell us where to hit it."

Mason tapped the pad several times before shaking his head. "I'm not really seeing any weak points. If the mini-gun overheats it will start popping the kernels. That seems to be the biggest beef on the forums. Actually, that could be kind of fun."

"Nothing else?"

Mason searched the information. "No. It's weatherized. But that shouldn't be a problem for our disruptors."

"Good," Jake said. "Let's make this takedown quick. And take it easy on the equipment. Don't pull the trigger any more than you have to. Most of all, stay safe."

Kat spoke to Jake without taking her eyes off the road. "If this thing is so new, why did they call us?"

"The warranty team gave them a window of several days before they could come. I guess the farm decided that stopping a robot's murderous rampage was something that couldn't wait."

"We don't get many of those anymore."

"Corporate calls or owners with a conscience?"

"Yes." Kat pulled onto the exchange and followed the ramp onto another freeway. A small car swerved out of the way, waking its sleeping passenger.

It was another hour on interstates, highways and farm-to-market roads before the truck turned down the mile long driveway that led to the farm. Corn grew in fields on either side and Jake watched the stalks sway in the gentle, late-day breeze.

He rolled the window down to let the smell of the field into the car and the smell of the car out. Cold air blew in. He fought back a shiver as Kat pulled into a parking lot and stopped the Beast beside a black SUV that was only a fraction smaller and newer than the Travelall.

She killed the engine and waited for it to ping to a stop. She pointed to the black truck and spoke. "I thought you said they weren't coming."

Jake watched as the door to the truck opened and a woman stepped out into the chilly night air. She shivered and pulled on a windbreaker bearing the ZUMR Robotics logo. She smiled at Jake and shut her door.

"Hey, that's…" began Glitch.

"What's this bullshit?" Mason asked.

"Wait here." Jake turned to Kat. "All of you. I'll see what's up."

The Travelall door squeaked as it opened and clanged as he forced it shut behind him.

"Your team can turn around, Jake," the woman said. "ZUMR will handle this."

"The hell you will."

"It's our equipment, Jake."

"It's our call, Hailey. You left them hanging." He smiled for the first time. "Which doesn't surprise me at all."

Her smile faded. "Well, I'm here now."

"You certainly are." He looked over her shoulder. He knew she was hiding long and rich dark hair beneath her corporate cap. He knew it smelled like warm coconut. He shut out the memory. "But where's your team?"

A whirring sound came from inside her truck and a small robot emerged from the window. No bigger than a coffee can, the Whir-bert flew on small rotors and bleeped and blooped as it perched on Hailey's shoulder.

"Your team's gotten smaller since the last time," Jake said.

"They'll be here. There was some kind of mix-up at dispatch."

"Sure there was."

Before she could respond, a door to one of the office buildings flew open and a man in a suit jogged across the parking lot to the couple. He steered toward Hailey and stuck out his hand. "Ashley?

Thank God."

The woman put out her own hand.

Jake stepped in front of her. "I'm Ashley." He tried to intercept the handshake.

The man in the suit pulled his hand back. "You're Ashley?"

"Yes, sir."

The man offered his hand again, but with some obvious hesitation.

"Is there a problem?" Jake asked.

"I guess I just expected someone less mannish."

Hailey laughed at this.

"Jake Ashley," he said with emphasis on the Jake. "We're here to help you with your malfunctioning equipment."

"Oh, I see. I'm Dan Forester. I'm sorry. I'm sure that happens quite a bit."

"It does," Hailey said with a laugh.

"You're probably used to it then."

Jake shook his head. "You'd think so."

Forester turned to the woman with the robot on her shoulder. "So, are you with him?"

"Hardly." Hailey stepped in front of Jake and took the man's hand. "Hailey Graves. ZUMR Robotics, Warranty department."

"But, I thought you couldn't be here. I was told you couldn't be here."

"They aren't," Jake said. "Miss Graves is alone. My team is here and we're ready to go."

"My team will be here shortly," Hailey argued.

"But it's moving." There was panic in the corporate famer's

voice. "I told your company this, Miss Graves. We don't want it to harm anyone else."

She nodded where she was supposed to nod, made a sad face at the sad parts and then responded with practiced confidence. "My team should be here in an hour, Mr. Forester."

"An hour!" Forester and Jake joined together in their disbelief.

"It could be gone in an hour, Miss Graves," Jake said. "We need to take care of this menace right now."

Whir-bert looked at Jake and blasted a series of angry bleeps.

Hailey protested as well. "Sir, if you'll just be patient, ZUMR will handle this situation."

"And what is the reward for his patience, Miss Graves?" Jake asked. "How many more have to die? And how many stories have to be written about all those dead bodies that piled up while we just stood here and waited?"

"Jake," she hissed.

Jake turned back to the man in the suit. "We can have this taken care of in no time, Mr. Forester."

"Any actions taken by an independent contractor will void the machine's warranty." How she loved to lecture.

Dan Forester cared about people. That was obvious. But the talk of capital investments shook his principles. Jake could see the hems and haws coming. He had to get in front of them.

"Warranty?!" Jake said. "How can you think about warranties at a time like this, Miss Graves? What is the cost of a single machine versus a human life?"

Forester wrung his hands together. "Quite a lot actually."

"Is it more than the price of integrity?" Jake asked.

Forester shrugged with a nervous smile.

Hailey showed Jake an invoice.

Jake nodded. "Fair enough. That is a lot. But is it more than the price of a PR team to keep Happy Dell Independent Family Farms Incorporated off the news streams?"

The man sighed. "Please take care of the matter, Mr. Ashley."

Jake turned to the Beast and yelled. "We're up!"

The doors opened and the crew filed out of the truck. They moved to the rear and began unloading their gear.

"You unctuous jerk," Hailey said under her breath.

"I've asked you before, please don't insult me with words I have to look up. We don't have time for that. We have to stop this killer." Jake started for the truck.

"You're a prick," she said louder.

He turned. "There. Wasn't that easier?"

Forester followed. "So, we're all good now, right? I can go? Home? You'll call when it's done?" The executive farmer turned to leave.

"Mr. Forester, before you go, there is one thing I have to ask you."

"Yes?" He bounced on the balls of his feet. Each bounce took him closer to the safety of his car.

"Has the machine ever exhibited any artistic qualities?" Jake asked.

"What... what do you mean?"

"Has it ever written you a poem? Sung a song? Written a book?"

"No."

Mason popped his head around the corner of the truck. "And it just shot the employee? It didn't dress him up like a scarecrow and put him on a stake?"

"What?" Forester squirmed. "No!"

"It didn't pin a sign to him that said, 'If I only had a brain'?"

"No! My God. Why are you asking this?"

"It's just something we have to do, Mr. Forester." Jake said. "Sentience complicates things. But it sounds like we're in the clear."

Forester looked more frightened by it all than annoyed by the technicalities. "Can I go?"

"Yeah," Mason said. "You can run away now."

Dan Forester nodded and jogged to his car. He slammed the vehicle's door and sped away.

Mason held up Jake's disruptor pack and motioned for him to turn around.

"'If I only had a brain'?" Jake asked.

"And then the robot takes the brains out of the farmer's head. That's poetic justice, Jake. Which is a form of poetry, and poetry is art."

"You know why no one likes you, right?"

"Yep." Mason held up the pack again.

Jake slipped his arms into the shoulder straps and switched on the pack. He pulled the discharger from the holster and checked the safety. It was broken.

3

They stood at the edge of the cornfield, staring down the rows of the golden green crop as the sun began to set. The breeze danced through the field and the stalks swayed at its command. The motion and the darkness made it difficult to detect any movement that wasn't corn.

Jake didn't like it. "Send up the drone, Mason."

"What drone?" Mason asked.

"What do you mean, 'what drone'?"

"You mean the Seeker 4000 with thermal imaging and focal plane arrays capable of detection and pursuit?"

"Of course I mean that one."

"Ah, well then you would also mean the one that is sitting in thirty-two separate parts back at the office waiting on a new focal plane array, firmware realignment and a valid operator's permit."

"Perfect."

A gust of wind startled the cornfield and the stalks dipped further into the rows. A dozen shrill whistles rose from the field.

"Do you all hear that?" Glitch put a hand to his ear and made an adjustment on a knob hidden behind his earlobe. "What's that sound?"

"That's the wind whipping through the plains," Mason said.

"What?"

Mason stared at the cyborg. "Didn't you ever blow on a blade of grass?"

Glitch shook his head.

Mason grumbled, "Stupid kids," before saying, "It whistles." He pointed to the field. "Like that."

"Oh, good. I thought my ear was buggy again. I think a wire is loose."

"Does any part of you work?" Mason asked.

"My fist works. Want me to show you?"

Kat stepped between them. "Knock it off, the both of you. We don't want this thing sneaking up on us just because you two can't keep your mouths shut."

"We'd never hear it anyway," Mason said. "This thing has sound baffling like you wouldn't believe."

"For a scarecrow?" Kat asked.

"The thing was designed to sneak up on birds, Kat. And a

crow's hearing is better than a human's. And way better than Glitch's, apparently."

"Shut up, Mason. I can hear you, you know."

"Perfect." Jake ignored them both and peered into the rows of corn. He turned his head, listening for the silent killer. "So we can't see it. And we can't hear it. Any good news?"

"Yeah, since it doesn't really matter, I can keep on insulting ED-Four O Nine pounds here."

"Hey," was Glitch's only comeback.

"Seriously, Glitch?" Mason shook his head. "Is there anyway you can upgrade your wit? Because you're just making things too easy for me."

"Just shut up and let me think." Jake paced the edge of the cornfield, peering down each row as far as the darkness would allow.

Kat stepped beside him and asked quietly, "What are you thinking?"

"I'm thinking it couldn't be much worse. A silent renegade machine equipped for killing and hiding in a maze of noisy darkness."

"I don't want to be the one to say it, but you could hand it over to Hailey and her team."

Jake turned back to the team. "Here's the plan. We'll split up—"

"Because that always works," Mason said.

"Shut it, Mason," Jake said.

"No, really, I saw it in a horror movie once."

"Enough." Jake walked to the head of a corn row. "We'll split up. But keep no more than one row between us and stay abreast of each other at all times."

Mason held up a finger and opened his mouth.

"And no abreast jokes," Jake finished.

Mason closed his mouth and lowered his hand.

"Mason, hand out the comms."

"What comms, Jake?"

Jake closed his eyes and took a deep breath. "Fine. Keep an ear out for one another and have their back. This isn't your typical murderous laundry machine. It's quiet, has a machine gun for one arm and a sword for the other. It's dangerous. Let's find it and put it down quick."

The team nodded and spread out across the edge of the cornfield.

The discharger was shaped like a small carbine and he pulled if from a holster on his hip. He pulled the stock to his shoulder and made sure the cable that ran from the pommel was free of obstruction. His thumb found the safety and switched it off as if it actually worked in the first place. Within seconds, the pack on his back warmed as the circuits closed and the capacitor charged. A pull of the trigger would send the disruption charge through the baton and out a directional Tesla coil at the end of the instrument.

A single charge could incapacitate most consumer and low-end industrial models. The R34-P3R was weatherized, however, and Jake questioned how effective it would actually be. He looked over to Glitch.

Each team member carried a similar backpack, but the giant cyborg had another tool slung across his back. The cannon looked like a rifle built to ridiculous proportions. The barrel could double for a sewer pipe, and the receiver was a block the size of a car battery. Its bulk made it too cumbersome for anyone that wasn't augmented like Glitch.

Glitch caught Jake's look and acknowledged the stare.

Jake nodded. "Keep the IMP handy."

Glitch nodded back and stepped into the cornfield. The rest followed his lead and each team member took a row.

Jake wasn't but a few feet in when the sounds of nature swallowed the footsteps of his teammates. Having never had the opportunity to wander through a cornfield, Jake had always pictured them as quiet, serene places, but the snap of the stalks and crackle of the plants made it anything but relaxing. Every creak could be their prey, every snap could be an ambush, and every sound put his nerves on edge.

The ground was moist beneath his feet and rich with an earthy smell that rose with every cautious step. He moved slowly, straining to hear in the darkness.

A gust of wind pushed the crop deep into the furrowed row. He jumped back and gripped the disrupter tighter in his hand. Two rows over he heard Glitch swear. Four rows over he heard the faint traces of Mason laughing at Glitch's discomfort.

The wind calmed and for a brief moment Jake could see further into the crop. Something was there and it was staring back at him.

Maybe.

It was as tall as the crop itself and thin like a stalk but, unlike the corn, it didn't sway.

A shout rose in his throat but before it could escape his mouth, another gust of wind obscured his view. He held still and waited for the wind to rest. When it did, he peered once more into the darkness at what he thought he had seen. But it wasn't there. He shuddered.

"It's ahead of us," he called to either side.

"Where?" Glitch's voice was faint in the field of plants.

"I don't know."

"Real helpful!" Mason screamed back. "Thanks."

Jake walked faster, calling for positioning every few meters to make sure the team was keeping together. The wind came in spurts and slowed their progress. It soon became almost rhythmic. With every pause, Jake scanned the field for the shadowy figure. But shadows were everywhere and he could never be certain the movement he spotted was anything other than corn.

Another gust blew a mass of leaves in his face. He grabbed at the plant. "I'm starting to really hate corn," he shouted and swatted the plant away.

It was in front of him. An evil face etched in metal beneath a rotting, floppy hat.

Jake screamed and stumbled backward as the machine swung its left arm.

He fell beneath the scythe as it cut a silver arc through air and corn. He hit the ground and the sliced plants crashed down on top of him.

The machine held up its left arm and glanced at an ear of corn impaled on the long and slender blade. The Reaper raised its arm to strike again.

Jake pulled the disruptor's trigger. A blue burst of voltage lit the field around him and crackled through the air as the arc connected with the tip of the scythe.

The arm stopped. The blade shuddered. The speared corncob popped.

The appendage fell dead at the scarecrow's side, but the robot did not fall. The machine looked at the dead limb and tried to move it again. Its torso bucked but the arm would not respond other than flopping a bit.

"It's here!" Jake shouted.

A whir filled the cornrow and the Reaper raised its other arm. The kernel cannon's barrels blurred as they spun up to speed.

Jake scrambled back on knees and elbows.

The scarecrow fired.

Plumes of earth chased him backward as the kernels spit from the mini-gun and dug into the ground. They stitched the earth closer and closer until they had reached just below his feet.

Jake fired again. The disrupter's charge leapt to the floating barrels but did nothing to stop their spin. The arm did not fall.

The Reaper continued to fire.

The musky smell of damp earth was quickly overtaken by the scent of ozone and freshly popped popcorn as the fluffy white snack poured from the barrels and began to pile up on the ground.

An explosion of cornstalks erupted next to the machine as Glitch charged through the rows shoulder-first at the Reaper. The giant man plowed into the machine, lifting it from the ground and sending it several rows deep back into the field.

The cyborg glanced at Jake quickly and dove into the field

after the machine.

"Glitch, wait." Jake started to get to his feet as Mason and Kat found their way through the web of leaves.

Kat grabbed Jake's hand and helped him up as Mason grabbed a handful of popcorn off the ground.

"Where did they go?" Kat asked.

Jake pointed down the row. "Follow the wreckage."

"Did yoush mape dish, Jakgh? Dish ish delicishous," Mason said through a mouthful of popcorn. "Neesh buttersh sthow."

Jake and Kat forced Mason toward the new path that Glitch had cleared through the field. It twisted and turned in indiscriminate directions.

Fallen stalks tripped at their heels. The uneven nature of the furrowed field grabbed at their toes. More than once, Mason almost choked on his popcorn. For five minutes they rushed after their coworker, shouting his name as they fought to remain on their feet.

The path cut right, and they were met with a wall of corn. The team nearly fell over Glitch. The large man sat tenderly picking at his arm. His sleeve was dark with blood and he twitched with every touch.

"Glitch?" Kat put a hand on his shoulder.

"Damn thing shot me in my real arm."

"Are you okay?"

"Of all the arms I've got, he had to shoot this one."

"I'm sorry, Glitch," Kat said.

"Ah, it's okay. I was thinking about getting it replaced anyway."

"Why didn't you fry him?" Mason asked.

"I did. Right after he shot me." Glitch stood and brushed at the wounds on his arm. "Stupid thing used that spinny-gun to soak up the shot. Then he shot a bunch of popcorn at me and ran off."

"It's mini-gun, Glitch."

"Whatever it is. He's using it as a shield."

"It did the same back there," Jake said. "Mason. Kat. If you're going to shoot, try and hit it from the left side." He turned to Glitch. "Can you handle the IMP?"

Glitch pulled the large rifle from his back, seated it in his hand and smiled.

"Good. Try to keep the damage down." Jake turned to the others. "We distract. Glitch melts." He turned back and parted the corn. "Oh, thank God."

The team stepped through the crop into a large clearing. The heart of the farm consisted of several large steel barns surrounding a paved lot filled with equipment. Several service lights glowed above each door. It was the first light they'd seen since venturing into the fields. Unfortunately it didn't produce much more than atmosphere and shadows.

The group stepped onto the pavement and surveyed the area looking for movement or any clue as to where the machine had run.

"Any ideas?" Kat asked.

Mason raised his disruptor and started walking. "He went this way."

"How can you tell?"

He pointed to a trail of fluffy white popcorn. "Come on

Hansel. Come on Gretel."

There wasn't much, but the wind had left enough of the popcorn undisturbed to establish a trail.

"Everyone stay behind Glitch." Jake spoke softly.

"That's because he likes you least," Mason said.

"It's because of the IMP, you jerk."

"Shut up, both of you," Kat said. "Before the wind takes the trail away."

The crew formed up behind the cyborg's bulk in a small "V" as Glitch followed the white specks.

They had taken only a few steps when a sound in the cornfield had them all spinning on their heels. Glitch pulled the trigger on the IMP and it kicked in his hands. The sound it made was subtle, a high-pitched *bloop* like a pebble falling into a hundred-foot well, but the shot itself tore a four-foot hole straight through the crop.

The stalks that weren't obliterated burned. The kernels popped all at once, creating a cloud of popcorn. Once it settled to the ground, it looked like Christmas and the team could see clear through to the other side of the cornfield.

There was nothing else behind them.

Mason clapped. "Nice shot, Redenbacher."

"Shut up, Mason."

He patted Glitch on the belly. "Whatever you say Jiffy-Puffy."

"I'm not fat. They're servos."

"Yeah, okay."

"Would you two please just follow the trail before the wind blows it away?" Kat asked.

"Right." Mason pointed ahead of Glitch. "Follow the popcorn.

Like a professional."

The still air didn't last long, but it didn't have to. The popcorn led them around the corner to a metal barn that was larger than most neighborhoods. Once they turned the corner, they found the steel door ripped from its hinges and tossed ten feet away.

"I think he went in there," Glitch said.

"Very good, Glitch." Mason asked. "That new processor is really doing wonders for you."

Jake shook his head and stepped through the hole into the barn. He reached out to the wall looking for a light switch, not really expecting it to be there. It wasn't. The barn felt even bigger inside. He pulled out a flashlight and hit the switch.

The beam didn't penetrate far into the darkness, but the cavernous nature of the barn was exposed. It rose three stories up before there was anything resembling a ceiling and was filled with massive pieces of farm equipment. Several harvesters were lined up near a pair of monstrous doors. They were set to roll as soon as the computers said the crop was ready.

The rest of the team filed in behind Jake and spread out along the wall.

Jake splashed the flashlight around the group. "Someone find the lights."

Before anyone could respond with a "how?" or "yeah right" the metal cavern filled with a mechanical whir.

"Spinny-gun!" Glitch shouted and shoved Mason out of the way a half second before the corn came raining down from the rafters.

Mason hit the ground as the rest of the crew dove for cover.

Glitch stood. The big man's machine mind snapped on. As the corn struck the floor around him, one of his oddmentations began to calculate the trajectory of the corn and triangulated its origin in the darkness.

The data load was immense due to the number of kernels, but it finally returned an answer.

"I've got you now," Glitch said as he raised the IMP and fired. The gun sounded and a round section of the roof melted away, letting in just enough moonlight to expose the Reaper's silhouette as the machine leapt from its place in the rafters.

The IMP was knocked from Glitch's hands as the mechanical scarecrow kicked the giant back against one of the harvesters.

The Reaper's left arm still hung limp at its side, but it swung the mini-gun barrel to great effect, bashing Glitch back into the machine every time he took a step forward.

"Shoot it!" Mason yelled as he searched for his disruptor.

Kat kept tabs on the Reaper with her own disruptor but couldn't get a clear shot. "The current will run right through it into Glitch."

Jake stepped out from behind a crate and the mini-gun spooled up instantly to fire. He dove back behind cover as the kernels dug into the wood.

Glitch made the most of the momentary distraction and seized the machine by the waist. The metal muscles in his arm twitched as he lifted the Reaper above his head. He bashed it into the ground as he yelled, "You hurt my real arm!"

The Reaper's eyes turned brighter and it brought the gun to bear on the cyborg. Then its head and torso melted.

Mason flew back across the room and dropped the IMP as he slammed into the barn wall and collapsed.

The collision caused the entire structure to roll like thunder.

Glitch dropped the remains of the machine and rushed to his side. "Are you okay, Mason?"

Jake slid to his knees and examined Mason as best he could. "Would someone find the lights?"

"I'm on it." Glitch stood and ran off into the darkness.

"Firing the IMP?" Jake said. "That was…"

"Brave. Courageous. Selfless." Mason said as he stood on shaky legs.

"Stupid," Jake said.

"This sounds an awful lot like the start of one of your insurance premium rants."

"You're an idiot."

"Oh, now we're doing performance reviews?"

Bright lights filled the barn with a boom.

"Good job, Glitch," Jake shouted over his shoulder.

Glitch's voice came back from somewhere deep in the barn. "That wasn't me."

Jake turned. The lights weren't coming from overhead. They were coming from one of the massive combines. The work lights were focused on the two men in front of the barn doors.

"That's weird and terrifying," Mason said.

"Maybe it's just trying to help," Jake said not believing a word of it.

"Yeah, I don't like the way it's looking at us."

"I'm sure it's just the farmers back at the office trying to help." Why did he keep saying things he didn't believe?

The combine's engine turned over and the giant machine began to rumble. The blades began to spin.

"How sure are you?"

Jake started to edge toward the access door they had entered. "Not much. Actually I kind of regret saying it because now it sounds really stupid."

The combine lurched forward as the two men dove aside. It crashed into the door and produced a thunderclap that shook the barn and rattled the team.

Glitch ran out of the darkness and joined the two men. "What did you guys do?"

The combine backed up and redirected its lights at the trio.

"Run!" Mason shouted and turned for the door.

Jake and Glitch followed.

The three men ran out of the barn and were halfway across the tarmac when the combine exploded through the barn doors in a shower of sparks and screeching metal. The combine's reel snapped in two and spun away across the parking lot. The machine turned on the fleeing trio and choked out the moon with its work lights.

Jake fired a blast from the disruptor, knowing that it would do little to slow the massive machine. The streak of electricity ran the length of the farm equipment to no effect.

They zigged and zagged across the open space and the machine course-corrected each time.

Cybernetics notwithstanding, Glitch's bulk slowed him down and he was falling behind. "It's following us."

"You think, dumbass?" Mason shouted as he tried his own disruptor against the machine. It worked as well as Jake's.

"Lose it in the corn," Jake yelled and turned into the field.

Glitch followed him as Mason took the next row over.

"I'm not going to make it, guys." Glitch yelled.

"You can do it, Glitch." Jake turned to encourage him. "Redirect power or something."

"Nope." Glitch crashed to the ground and slid through the dirt as the combine tore into the corn behind him. "I was right."

The machine sucked the giant man into its maw and Glitch's screams disappeared inside the machine.

Jake screamed himself and fired his disruptor at the combine until the system shut down to prevent it from overheating.

The machine chewed through the corn toward him.

Mason burst through the row of stalks and fired his own weapon to failsafe.

The machine kept coming.

The two men turned to run but bounced off one another in the process and fell to the ground.

The combine's blades snapped at a blurring rate as they neared, and the two men kicked into the dirt trying to push themselves away.

The machine loomed over them.

The lights were blinding them.

The two men rolled out of way as the blades sheared the corn stalks from the earth and the combine passed between them.

Jake got to his feet and beat against the machine looking for a hollow spot, a belly in the beast. He screamed the cyborg's name.

"Glitch!"

"I'm okay." The voice came from behind the combine.

Jake rushed to the rear of the machine and found Glitch lying in the cleared field naked to the skin.

"Glitch! Glitch, are you okay?" Jake asked.

"Yeah. I think so."

"How the hell are you okay?!"

Mason ran around the far side and saw the two men. "Why are you naked?"

"That thing ate my clothes." Glitch stood, revealing that every shred of material had been thrashed away on his journey through the machine. Also, that his crotch glowed in the dark.

"Geez, Glitch. Even your junk? Can't you leave anything alone?"

"Shut up, Mason."

"Let's talk about Glitch's little light show later," Jake said. "It's turning around."

The combine roared as it turned and bore down upon them once more.

"Man that thing is surprisingly nimble." Mason checked the status on his disruptor.

Jake held up his own and saw that it was ready to fire once more. "Maybe if we both hit it at once?"

"Sure," Mason nodded enthusiastically, "that will never work."

"Just shoot."

Both men fired and the front of the combine turned blue as the disruptors let flow a steady stream of electric bursts. The engine sputtered, wheezed and died, leaving them in silence but for their panting and something on Glitch that beeped.

The work lights flickered, popped and went out leaving them in the dark with only their flashlights and Glitch's junk providing any kind of light.

Mason looked at the weapon in his hand. "That really shouldn't have worked."

The combine boomed and all three men jumped. A hatch squeaked open and Kat jumped to the ground. "It looks like I saved you all once— Glitch, why is your dick glowing?"

4

Bruises and fatigue made it a long walk back for everyone, but even more so for Glitch, as the tarp they'd found in the barn covered his nakedness but did little to hide the glow in his crotch.

"Tell me it's just to make peeing at night easier."

"Shut up, Mason."

"I'm not judging," Mason said. "Just asking."

"No, you're judging."

"Okay, you're right. I'm judging."

They reached the office parking lot to a round of applause.

The rest of the ZUMR team had arrived and were busy

unloading their reclamation equipment. Four robots standing seven feet tall and four wide at the chest stomped into the parking lot from an old model moving truck. Designed to take a beating from anything the company had ever manufactured, they were built thick and shook the ground when they walked.

The technicians turned at the team's approach and clapped fervently, whistled and made other congratulatory comments that they obviously didn't mean in the least.

Mason told them all to go to hell and walked back over to the Beast.

Hailey didn't clap, but she was smiling when she walked up to Jake. "How did it go, Jake?"

"It went fine."

"You have a funny definition of fine, Ashley." The man's name was Colton Porter. And he was a dick.

He walked up to the couple and held up his phone. A splintered ray of light shot from the end, projecting a large screen into the air that was playing drone footage of the exact moment Glitch was dropped naked from the combine into the cornfield. "So that's how morons are born. So much for the cabbage patch."

The ZUMR technicians laughed at this.

Glitch turned red and rushed to the Beast, where he sat inside wrapped in his tarp and sulked.

"You're a class act, Colton," Jake said.

"Sorry, Ashley. I wasn't thinking." He put his arm around a reclamation bot and smiled. "You see, our machines don't have feelings. They just do what they're told and keep their pants on."

"You put a little too much faith in your machines. I wouldn't trust them to fold my laundry, much less stand by me in the field when it mattered. One little hiccup and I've got two renegades to worry about."

"That's not how it works, junker. A machine can't turn other machines."

"Don't be so sure."

"I wouldn't expect you to understand." He patted the machine on the back. "I coded the Guardian series myself. They are completely incorruptible and incapable of anything but compliance."

"Yay for you. I'll remember that the first time I'm called to bring one down."

"You wouldn't stand a chance."

Jake smiled at Colton and took Hailey by the arm. He led her a few feet away under protest.

"What are you doing?" She snapped her arm out of his hand.

"I need to talk to you about something. How long did you have your drone overhead? How much did you see?"

"I saw it all. You managed to destroy a barn, a crop, a combine and Glitch's pants all in a few minutes. I'd call it your highlight reel."

"You saw it then?"

"Saw what?"

"The second anom."

"What? No, there was no second anomaly."

"Then what do you call that giant corn cob chomping monster that tried to run us down?"

"If I had to guess, I'd say salvage error."

"You think we turned it on ourselves?"

"Oh, I'm sure it was an accident." She put air quotes around "accident." He hated it when she used air quotes. "I'm sure a stray shot probably triggered its programming. And I say that because I'd never accuse you of intentionally sabotaging a machine just to justify a second bounty."

"You'd never do that? That's sweet of you."

Hailey nodded. "Just like I'd never even think for a half a second that you would fry a machine and make it go renegade just to extort more money out of the poor farmers here at Happy Dell Independent Family Farms Incorporated."

"Isn't that nice of you to say."

She smiled at him and nodded.

He leaned in close. "Look, you and I can play I Hate My Ex all night long, but I'm being serious here."

She folded her arms and cocked her hip. "Yeah, because you're Mr. Serious."

"Hailey, we never touched it. Not once. It went renegade on its own. I swear."

"First of all," she said. "We are not exes. We would have to have been a thing before we could even be a couple. And we'd have to be a couple before we could be exes. That's how it works. And you and I were never a thing. You get me? Second of all, you don't get to swear. I get to swear. If anyone has a right to swear it's me, dammit."

Jake took a deep breath, focused on removing all sarcasm from his voice and looked her in the eyes. "Hailey, both of them were ZUMR tech. Don't you think that's at least worth looking into? At the very least to cover your company's ass?"

Hailey looked away and sighed.

"Look," Jake continued, "I want to be wrong. And I want you to be the one that proves me wrong. Because I know how much you'd enjoy that. So please, prove me wrong and call me up and tell me you told me so."

She looked at the ground and ran her fingertip over her lip as she thought. Then she nodded. "I'll look into it."

"That's all I ask." Jake turned and stepped toward the truck. His mind was working on how to explain everything to Forester.

"Jake," Hailey called with no trace of hate.

This surprised him and he turned. "Yes?"

"Thank you," she said.

And she meant it. He could tell. His heart tripped and tried to tell him all of the things that her tone could possibly mean because it wasn't what she said, it was how she said it.

So, how did she say it? She had said it softly. That could mean she didn't want others to hear, which wasn't necessarily a good or bad thing.

How was she standing? That mattered. Body language was ninety percent of communication. It was open. She had unfolded her arms. That meant she wasn't opposed to further communication. That was a good thing.

How was she dressed? That mattered, too. She was in a one-piece blue ZUMR jumpsuit, which meant that she was working and he had lost all perspective on the conversation and was possibly going crazy and why did she have this effect on him?

And how long had he been staring now? Oh, no, he was well

beyond thoughtful pause and considered silence and was moving deep into awkward moment territory. He had to say something. "Hey, Hailey?"

"Yes, Jake?"

Something playful, but nothing serious. "Were we at least an item?"

"Good night, Jake." She turned and went back to her truck.

He watched her walk away and sighed. He decided to bill the farm first thing in the morning. He hoped they paid quickly. Hopefully before they came back out here and saw the damage that had been done. But it could wait until morning. He just wanted to go home.

5

The next morning arrived as it normally did. Some embraced it. Others cursed it. And for a lucky few who got to sleep through it, the morning crept on by without making any kind of fuss at all. Jake neither embraced nor feared mornings. They happened. That was enough for him.

He was still rubbing the stiffness out of his back when he opened the door to the shop. The idea of getting paid would have excited him, but he knew it would be months before the Happy Dell Independent Family Farms Incorporated account was settled.

The combine had to be explained, documented, argued,

probably litigated and eventually settled for a fraction of the original charge. If they were lucky, they might get something for the night's work in the end. Maybe salvage rights. The runaround was fully expected.

What he didn't expect was that he'd open the door to a rousing speech being given by a beautiful woman. That almost never happened.

The crew was gathered on the shop floor in front of the woman. She was standing next to Uncle Aaron on the stairs to the office and speaking to the gathering of four as if it were a crowd of thousands. "...don't let anyone tell you otherwise, you are all heroes. Your work is a benefit to all of humanity. What you do, every day, is ensuring that humankind remains the dominant species on Earth. You are not just saving lives, you are saving the entire human race."

The woman heard the door close and turned toward the sound.

"Hey, Jake." Savant had returned, apparently, and waved him over. "Come here. This lady is saying nice things about us."

"She isn't saying nice things about you, Savant," Glitch said. "You weren't even there."

"Why don't you say nice things about us, Jake?" Mason asked.

"Give me a reason, Mason."

The woman rushed down the steps toward him. She looked to be about forty, but anyone of means looked to be about forty. That's what a million dollars in science would get you at any doctor's office. Forty was the best science could do and it had been that way for years.

There was a new ad running for a surgeon that promised thirty-nine for $999,999.99, but most everyone considered it a gimmick.

"There he is. There he is." The woman was all smiles and jiggles as she crossed the room with outstretched arms and Jake soon found himself in an uninvited hug that he wasn't all that upset about. Science did good work.

Uncle Aaron crossed the room behind her and let the hug finish. "Jake, I'd like you to meet Meagan Mouret."

"It's wonderful to meet you, Jake. Your uncle has nothing but wonderful things to say about you."

Her smile was warm and so practiced that Jake almost bought it. "Well, thanks, Uncle Aaron. It's nice to meet you, Meagan. Now if you don't mind, we're a little busy around here today."

"Doing what?" Kat asked.

Jake's lip stiffened. "How about repairing everything that broke last night?"

Glitch rolled his head like a distraught toddler. "Aw, we can do that later. She was saying such nice things about us. She called us heroes, Jake. Heroes."

"Why don't you ever call us heroes, Jake?" Mason asked.

"It's true," Meagan said. "All of it. You're all heroes. Just think of all the lives you potentially saved by destroying that menace last night. You're doing great work for humanity."

"You hear that?" Glitch puffed out his chest. Something beeped. "Heroes of humanity."

Jake grunted. "I'm pretty sure we saved more crows than people."

"Heroes of crowmanity," Glitch said.

Mason rolled his eyes at the cyborg. "You're an idiot."

"Idiot of crowmanity," Glitch corrected.

Meagan laughed a rehearsed giggle. There was a hint of autotune in the laugh. "So cavalier. I love it. Even as soldiers in the great conflict you remain truly grounded."

"What great conflict?" Glitch asked before Jake could tell him not to.

Meagan smiled. "Make no mistake. You are fighting in a great war with nothing less at stake than human dominance over machines. Every robot you destroy, every evil contraption you put down is another blow for humankind."

Now Kat rolled her eyes. They landed on Jake with a look that said there were better things she could be doing.

"Wow. Humankind." Glitch gasped. "I had no idea."

Meagan continued to heap praise on Glitch while Jake grabbed Uncle Aaron by the shoulder and pulled him aside.

"Why is your girlfriend here?"

"She wanted to meet you. She loves the work you're doing."

"She's one of those anti-robot crazies."

"She's not a nut, Jake. She's a nice woman. Besides, you're anti-robot."

"I am not."

"You destroy them for a living."

"We handle malfunctioning equipment, plain and simple. We're hardly taking a moral stand when dealing with a broken dishwasher. Putting down a lawnmower that's invaded the neighbor's yard one too many times is hardly putting an ethical stake in the ground."

"You're right, okay. I don't care either. But what's the harm in letting her get excited? It doesn't hurt you any. And it goes a long way for me." Uncle Aaron planted an elbow in Jake's ribs.

Jake pulled away. "Fine. Let her say her piece and get her out of here. We're busy."

Aaron laughed. "That's a lie."

"She's distracting my team," Jake said.

"Fine, we won't take up any more of your precious time." Aaron practically cooed while looking at the woman. "Oh, I forgot. She wants to give you an award."

"An award? From her society? They're practically terrorists!"

Aaron put a finger in Jake's chest. "No, they're not, Jake. Terrorists are scary." He stepped aside and pointed to Meagan and turned back to Jake. "Look at that ass. There's nothing scary about it. It's all daydreams and happy thoughts. It makes me smile just thinking about it."

"Thinking about what, Aaron?" Meagan asked.

Aaron turned surprised to see Meagan had joined them. "Oh… the award."

"Aaron, I told you not to say anything."

"I couldn't help it, baby doll. I'm just so excited."

"Baby doll?" Jake felt a little sick.

Meagan pouted, but it was cute. Another practiced expression. She hit Aaron on the shoulder and smiled. "I didn't want him to ruin the surprise. My organization would like to present you an award for all of the wonderful work you're doing."

"That's really not necessary," Jake forced a smile. "We were just doing our jobs. There's no reason to make a fuss."

"Don't be silly. It's no fuss at all. It's just a small ceremony."

"A ceremony?" Jake looked at his uncle, who pleaded with his eyes not to screw this up for him.

"Of course, silly." Meagan smiled bigger and shook her head. "Heroes deserve an audience."

Jake put up his hands. "Absolutely not."

Meagan didn't even flinch. Her smile stayed in place. And somehow she said Aaron's name without even moving her lips.

Uncle Aaron dutifully sprang into action. "C'mon, Jake. It's the perfect thing to counter the bad press."

"What bad press?"

"Oh. You didn't know?" Aaron pulled his phone from his pocket and set it to project. The splintered lines filled the air and for the second time in less than twelve hours Jake was watching Glitch get depantsed by a farm combine.

"That son of a… Colton did this!"

Uncle Aaron read the username from the post. "It's someone called YourMom24482. Wow, he must have had that for a while to get such a low number."

"That sounds like him."

"Well, it's gone viral in the stream and they're laughing at you, Jake. They're laughing at our company."

"No, they're laughing at Glitch and his light-up junk."

Meagan put a hand on Jake's shoulder. "I heard all about what happened at the farm and I know that ZUMR is behind this. Those greedy bastards won't be happy until they drive every hard-working man and woman out of work. The ceremony would be a great way to paint you and your team as the underdog fighting the good fight against corporate greed. And, everyone loves an underdog."

"No, thank you," Jake said.

Aaron pointed to the video loop of Glitch's glowing junk. "Look at that, Jake. Our name's all over the place with this crap. Who's going to call us now?"

Jake shrugged. "No one was calling us before. We'll just wait and see what happens."

The phone in the office was wired to a bell in the shop. It rang and Aaron jumped. "How do you keep doing that?"

"Excuse me. I need to get that." Jake went up the stairs into the office and picked up the phone. "Ashley's Robot Reclamation and…" He sighed. They really needed a shorter name. "Junkers. Can I help you?"

"I always said you needed a shorter name," she said with a giggle.

"What do you want, Hailey?" Why was she calling him? Did this mean something? God, her voice sounded good. He had to remind himself that he was still pissed at her. "Calling to gloat?"

"I don't know what you're talking about."

"Right."

She giggled. "I don't know what you're so upset about. Glitch is a legend now."

"Do you think this is funny?"

"It is, and you know it is. But that wasn't me."

"No, it was that prick Colton."

"And he's been reprimanded. ZUMR does not condone that

kind of thing."

"Yeah I'm sure your boss is just tore up about the whole thing. What do you want, Hailey?"

"I want you to come to ZUMR. We have a job for you."

"Wow. Maybe they really do feel bad. Thanks, but no thanks. You know I won't go corporate."

"That's not the kind of job I'm talking about." Hailey's voice hardened. "It's about last night."

Jake looked at the broken clock in the wastebasket. It wasn't running but he could still hear the seconds ticking by as a thousand thoughts ran through his mind about the night before. The least of which had anything to do with robots.

"Will you come?" she asked.

Jake sighed and asked. "Will Colton be there?"

"You know he probably will."

"Fine. If I don't like what you have to say, I'm going to punch him."

"You could punch him anyway."

"Deal."

"Tell Glitch I said hi," she giggled again.

"You have no shame."

6

The ZUMR lobby was half waiting area, half museum. Glass cases, bronze plaques and full-blown prototypes showcased the history of the iconic company from freemium software startup to robotics empire.

A giant monitor formed a centerpiece in the mezzanine and played a continuous loop highlighting their early successful games: Bash of the Battalions, Sugar Saga Sort 'Em, Pissed Off Parrots and the most addictive solitaire game known to man, called Just One More Game.

Compulsive gameplay and a strategy of targeting OCD

treatment centers made them a microtransaction juggernaut that had quickly expanded into home and industrial robotics.

Their first robot was suspended in the air with a fancy arrangement of magnetic fields that kept the vacuum cleaner spinning in slow rotation. The ZUMR Sucka was the company's first automaton, and though it did very little, it sold an awful lot.

The ALI55 model domestic servant was the first in a long line of successful maid bots and was the true birth of modern robotics in people's homes. Designed to be sweet and compliant, the maid's only major flaw was its inability to fold fitted sheets. Asking it to do so would result in a complete system overload that required a full reboot. The ALI55 was now in its seventh generation and the flaw had been fixed. It still couldn't fold a fitted sheet, but inside of shutting down, the request was now met with a physics lecture on how it was an impossible task that could only be performed by wizards.

The GlassTastic line of dishwashers was a landmark for the ZUMR brand and automation history. Overnight, it had changed the way Americans didn't do dishes. It not only loaded itself, it also automatically got frustrated, pre-rinsed the dishes, and rearranged the shelves at least twice before starting the machine, taking this tiresome burden off of mothers everywhere.

It was also the first domestic robot that tried to kill someone. This fact wasn't part of the display, but it was something every junker knew all too well.

The GlassTastic's first killing glitch was considered nothing more than a programming error. Patches were uploaded to fix the bug and the public went on its way not washing dishes. When it happened several more times despite additional patches and firmware updates, ZUMR finally admitted that any machine given the complexity to perform human labor on any intuitive basis would bear the potential to go "renegade" and attempt to murder its operator.

Once this was discovered, and a national discussion was held, the public gave a collective shrug and agreed that, while the fact that a machine could go renegade of its programing and try to murder someone was concerning, it was unlikely that it would be anyone they knew, and taking the chance was still better than washing their own dishes.

With the public accepting this risk, the robotics companies, ZUMR included, agreed to expand their warranties to cover murderous tendencies, threatening behavior and creepy leering. Of course, when the warranties expired the owners were on their own.

As impressive and familiar as the home automaton models were, ZUMR's real genius was seen in its industrial line. Over the years, they had automated and robotized every major industry in the world.

Transportation, agriculture, manufacturing, aquatic amusement parks, government services, forestry, construction, animal husbandry and more had seen their efficiency rise and their workforces shrink. All thanks to ZUMR and their competitors.

Jake had been here before, and paid little attention to the displays as he made his way across the lobby to the reception desk. "I'm Jake Ashley to see Hailey Graves."

"Who are you with, sir?"

"Ashley's Robot Reclamation of Green Hill."

"All right, I'll…" the receptionist smiled. "Wait, you're the guys from the feed?" The receptionist touched a control pad on his desk and the ZUMR promotional loop stopped in the middle of a game of Pissed Off Parrots and began to play the video from the farm. "You work with this guy?"

Jake placed his head on the counter and groaned. "Just tell her I'm here."

The man behind the desk chuckled again as the lobby filled with laughter at the video. Then the whispers began as the rumor quickly spread that the man standing with his head on the desk was a part of it all.

For the first time since he'd known her, Hailey came quickly. She rushed across the lobby and swiped her palm over the reader to sign Jake into the building. She noticed the video playing on the lobby monitor and instructed the receptionist to turn it off.

"I'm sorry, Jake."

"What's this about, Hailey? Did you find something?"

She looked around the lobby and simply said. "Not here. Come with me."

They walked to an elevator bay and past several armed security guards. The car was waiting for them and they were alone once they stepped inside. She commanded it to the top floor and stepped to the back of the car.

"Are you going to tell me what's happening?"

"Jack wants to tell you."

"Jack? Jack who?" Then it dawned on him. "Jackson Fox, billionaire and founder of ZUMR and billionaire?"

"That's the guy. But he goes by Jack."

They rode in silence for a bit. She had really rushed to meet him. That mattered. He began to wonder what it meant when she thankfully broke the silence.

"How's Glitch?"

"He's weird. Always has been."

"I meant with the sudden fame."

"I'm not sure he's even processed it yet. But he'll be fine. If you don't want people to see your junk, you shouldn't make it glow in the dark. My dad used to say that."

Hailey smiled at this as the doors opened and they stepped into the CEO's reception area. An android behind the desk stopped playing solitaire long enough to acknowledge the couple. "Hello, Ms. Graves."

"Hello MAR-E. We're here to see Jack."

"Mr. Fox said to send you right in." She touched a switch on her desk and the doors opened to Jackson Fox's ridiculously oversized and opulent office.

"Thank you, MAR-E."

The machine nodded and went back to her solitaire game as they entered the room.

The man himself was seated at the head of a large table occupied by several bots with glowing faces that represented members of ZUMR's board. Jake even recognized a few from the news.

As soon as he saw Hailey, Fox stood and waved off the board. Their faces went blank as the signals were broken, and the robots slumped in their chairs to signify they were offline.

Jackson Fox walked across the room to meet the two new

arrivals. He had been at the CEO game for a long time. He looked to be about forty.

He reached the couple and shook Jake's hand. "Jack Fox. It's nice to meet you, Mr. Ashley."

Jake nodded and was about to speak when Jack turned his attention to Hailey and kissed her on the cheek. It was obviously not a European thing.

Jake pointed between the two. "No kiss for me?"

Fox backed away and gave an uneasy smile. "My apologies, Mr. Ashley. Hailey told me about your history together and I should have been more considerate. I didn't think how it might affect you and that's probably because I'm rich and generally don't care what people think."

Jake shrugged. "Well at least you're an honest asshole."

The CEO smiled. He stepped over to his desk and picked up a coffee mug that read "World's Best CEO." "But I do care what you think about our problem, Jake. And ZUMR needs your help. I need your help." He held up the mug and tapped it.

A drone buzzed in through the open doors and filled the mug with freshly brewed coffee.

Fox put a hand on Jake's shoulder and directed him farther into the office. "We've got a big season ahead of us and I don't want anything messing it up. It could be our biggest year ever. Just look at this. It's our latest invention." The CEO pointed at a chair.

"It's a chair."

"You bet your ass it's a chair."

"I've seen chairs before, Jack."

"Not like this you haven't. It's going to completely

revolutionize sitting. Try it." He shoved Jake down into the chair.

It was the most comfortable he had ever been in his life. "My, that is a fine sit."

"It's robotic."

"Duh."

Jack laughed.

"I'll admit, it is the best my ass has ever felt."

"Good. We designed it that way. The robotics are constantly measuring your posture, temperature, and posterior and processing the information. It constantly adjusts to make your ass as comfortable as possible. The casters are also intuitive electric drive motors so moving around is easier than traditional rolling."

"Wait. So, it's measuring my ass?"

"It's all about data, Jake. Data makes everything better. And not only does it make you more comfortable and relaxed, it tells me a lot about who I'm talking to. Right now I can tell your heartbeat is a little elevated, you're perspiring-so little you may not even know it-and you're a little…"

"Tense?"

"Puckered," Jack said. "It's okay to relax."

"I'm puckered because you just told me this machine is measuring my ass." Jake stood.

The chair sounded sad.

"Hailey said something about a job?"

"Yes." Jack stepped behind his desk and his fingers danced across the surface. The lights in the room dimmed and a hologram of the R34-P3R appeared close enough to Jake's face to make him flinch.

"Sorry about that." Jack's fingers danced some more before he stepped out from behind the desk. "Of course, you're aware that one of our Reapers went renegade last night."

"I think I remember."

Jack smiled and swiped his hand. The scarecrow was replaced by an image of the combine. "And you suspect a double anomaly since one of our Crop Boys tried to kill you and did in fact depants your friend on global media."

Jake's eyes narrowed. "Are you serious?"

"I'm sorry." Fox smiled. "I couldn't resist."

"Sure." Jake nodded with a smile. "Must be the asshole thing."

Jack smiled back and swiped his hand. "What you don't know is that ZUMR has seen a dramatic upswing in our machinery going renegade."

The image that appeared looked like a steel barrel with legs.

"A week ago a Cementurion 120 attacked a construction worker. Buried the poor bastard in his own foundation."

He swiped at the air again and a thin biped in a tux filled the air.

"Six days ago a TailorBot stabbed a customer to death in the fitting room with nothing but bobby pins."

Another swipe. Another machine.

"Five days ago a Cordell Series Dog Walker walked eighteen dogs into a kitten store."

He swiped his hand several times and read off a litany of machines and murders.

"A ZooKeep 500 let the tigers out. A MistaBarista blinded three with steamed milk. And a BookBot stamped a woman to death and shoved her into a card catalog drawer at a library."

"Sounds like you've got your hands full." Jake looked around the office and spotted a guitar. He walked over to it and picked it up. He began to strum. "Are you looking to contract out reinforcements?"

"No. So far Hailey and her team have been able to handle it. You, of course, beat us to the punch last night, but that's not our concern."

"It's the double anomaly," Jake said.

Hailey nodded. "Anomalies have never occurred this close together. And last night they happened within hours of one another."

"If you brought me here for my opinion, I'd say it's all a little creepy."

"It's more than creepy," Jack said. "It's very suspect."

"You're not going to give the Uprising speech are you? I wouldn't imagine the head of ZUMR being a convert."

"Of course not," Jack scoffed. "Those lunatics don't know what they're talking about. Sentience simply isn't possible. Neither is rebellion."

"So it's not sentience or a programming issue," Jake said. "But you have a pretty good idea what it is, don't you?"

Jack looked at Hailey. She closed her eyes and nodded. Jack nodded back. "It's sabotage, Mr. Ashley."

Jake laughed. "You think someone is tinkering with your toys."

"Exactly," Fox agreed.

"Why now?" Jake asked as he set the guitar down.

The CEO cast another look at Hailey.

She gave another reassuring nod.

"Look, Hailey trusts you, Jake. She hates you, but she trusts you. So I will, as well. What I'm about to tell you doesn't leave this office." He made several gestures in the air that Jake couldn't repeat if he tried, and the BookBot image disappeared. A moment later a new hologram appeared.

It had two legs, two arms, about a thousand guns and more than a few missile batteries strapped to it here and there. A solider was shown next to it for scale and, unless ZUMR had found a way to shrink humans, the machine was massive. Nearly four stories tall.

"This is Project Cupcake," Jack said with a fair amount of puffery.

"That's the stupidest name for a walking tank that I've ever heard," Jake said.

"Would you look for a walking tank in a file called Project Cupcake?" Jack asked. "I didn't think so, so shut up because I'm smarter than you."

Jake whistled and pointed to the image. "That is impressive. And very illegal. I thought military bots were limited to logistics and support."

"They are." Jack gave the image a spin with his hand and it turned. "But not for long. The treaties that govern robots on the battlefield are outdated. Hell, we signed that treaty with the State of Davionia. Davionia doesn't even exist anymore. Those agreements were made when only a few nations had the capability to field military robots. Now that everyone has access, it's no longer seen as an unfair advantage. They're about to be dissolved."

"And you're ready to swoop in and grab the first contract."

"I'd be a terrible CEO if I wasn't. And I'm not a terrible CEO, Jake." He held up a book featuring his face and the title *The World's Best CEO*. "We've got the machine ready to go, but even having the processor in the same building would be a violation of a whole lot of laws."

"And I imagine the other companies are in the same boat. So they're trying to make your machines look unreliable before the bidding opens."

The CEO nodded.

"That's quite a pickle you're in, Jack, but I don't see what it has to do with me."

"I need someone to help me look into this, to investigate it. To find out who is messing with my machines."

"So why not send Hailey?"

"I can't have anyone from my company digging around. I need someone who can operate under the radar. With no connection to us whatsoever."

"Look, if the machines were tampered with, it's murder. Get the cops involved."

Hailey shook her head. "There is no evidence of the machines being tampered with. Whoever is behind this knows what they're doing."

"The truth is, Jake, my competitors would never suspect you. They know I would never hire you in a million years."

"Thanks," Jake said with complete insincerity.

Hailey huffed, "That's not what he meant, Jake."

"No, that's what I meant," Jack said. "But that's why this plan is so brilliant."

Jake couldn't help but laugh. "Thank you, both of you. But I'm no detective. I'm just the guy that cleans up the mess when your shit breaks and you don't care anymore. Now, if you'll excuse me, I was told I could punch that asshole, Colton."

Jake moved to the door and was quickly joined by Hailey.

"Jake, please think about this," Jack said. "I know you need the money."

"Wait." Jake turned back. "You went straight to the wallet? You didn't even try to appeal to my better nature first?"

Jack shrugged. "We're under a time crunch here. I didn't want to waste my time with the innocent lives at stake bit."

Jake's phone rang and he dug into his pocket to get it. "Fair enough."

He looked at the display and answered the call. "What's up, Kat?" He let her speak for a moment, said, "I see," and pulled the phone from his ear. He stared at Hailey and looked back to the CEO.

"What is it?" Hailey asked.

"A ZUMR passenger train has gone renegade. Innocent lives are at stake."

7

Jake pushed open the doors of the ZUMR building and rushed down the steps to the street with Hailey close behind him.

"That's a government contract," she yelled as she raced to catch him. "Why did they call you?"

Jake reached the street and found his bike. Much like the Beast, it was highly illegal unless properly permitted. He was certain the permits had lapsed, but he was now glad he brought it.

"Isn't it obvious? Your mysterious saboteur is trying to make you look bad by bringing in the infamous junkers that have the most popular video on the feed." He couldn't get through most of it without laughing.

Hailey frowned. "I'm serious."

He straddled the bike and looked at her. "Hailey, they said the thing is full of people and blowing through lights, so the call is coming from public channels." He dropped the helmet on his head and told it to connect him with Kat. As he waited for the phone to ring, he told Hailey, "Call your team."

The sound of a screeching tire was a startling sound to many. Automation had taken the wheel of the family car years ago and it was a rare thing that the computer would ever lock up the brakes and leave elevens in the parking lot.

He gunned the engine and the rear wheel spun. The pedestrians nearby jumped back and covered their ears. Several gave him hateful looks as the tire finally bit and he took off.

"Jake?" Kat's voice filled his helmet.

"Who called this in?"

"No idea. But it's public endangerment. We have to respond, right?"

"That's the code." A runaway train would be hard for ZUMR to cover up in any case. But calling in a third party would take the PR out of ZUMR's hands altogether. He shook his head. He wasn't starting to believe there was a conspiracy, was he?

"What do you want us to do, chief?" Kat asked.

"Move to intercept the train. I'm en route on Ninth on the bike. Hailey is on it as well."

"On your bike?"

"No, on the job. Her team is on the job."

Savant broke in. "So this is going to be a regular thing then?"

"Just call me when you're close!" He disconnected the call and focused on traffic. He maneuvered the bike between the cars and delighted as their response systems recognized him as a threat and pulled out of his way. All he had to do was accelerate near a bumper and the car would dash to the side to let him through.

The passengers looked at him with a mixture of anger and awe. The bike was an oddity. Ever since laws had required cars to drive themselves, motorcycles had vanished from the road. It was simply no fun to ride a motorcycle someone else was driving.

Trains, however, had seen a huge growth in popularity. Driving had lost its appeal for many once control was taken out of drivers' hands, and the train's popularity had soared. It wouldn't be full at this time of day. But it would hardly be empty.

The city of Green Hill had an extensive public transit system that ran primarily on an elevated platform to keep it away from pedestrians and traffic. The Metro-Interstate Green Hill Transit Enterprise had never experienced an anomaly, and it had been years since MIGHTE experienced any kind of reported accident. This was thanks, somewhat, to system improvements but more so to the fact that the city no longer classified morons struck while walking on the tracks as accidents.

Jake passed under an elevated rail section as the train zoomed overhead. He turned right and followed on the surface streets.

He contacted Kat through his helmet. "I'm tailing it."

"We're on our way. What's it doing?"

The track curved and the train teetered as it struggled to hold onto the track. Jake followed the curve on the bike and realized the people on board must be terrified.

"It's really moving. And it's not stopping for anything," Jake said as he watched the train blow by a second stop. This wasn't right. He'd seen a lot of things go wrong with machines, but the timing of this was just too perfect.

The train sped up even more as the platform descended to meet the road.

"It's heading to ground level. What are the authorities doing to-"

The train crossed an intersection against the light and plowed through several cars that were trying to cross. The force of the impact tossed several into the air.

"Holy shit!" Jake cut hard to his right as one came crashing down in front of him. He cut back left to miss another passenger car that was spinning toward him. He straightened out to clear the intersection, then turned left and sped onto the tracks behind the train.

"What happened?" Kat yelled in his ear.

"It just took out several cars!"

"What? How?"

"It ran a light that should have been set to all stop. Something is not right. The cars didn't even try to get out of the way."

"Savant just said the cars' awareness systems should have prevented any kind of collision."

"Tell Savant 'duh' for me. And make it sound really sarcastic. Like he would."

She did and then asked with concern, "What is going on, Jake?"

Were Jack and Hailey right? What they were proposing was

ridiculous. But their scenario fit the situation a little too well. "I'm not sure, Kat. Where are you?"

"We're not far from your position."

Jake heard another series of collisions from the head of the train. A moment later he shot through another intersection littered with damaged cars and confused passengers. He passed through so fast that he couldn't tell if anyone was hurt. He'd be surprised if they weren't.

The train began to pull away.

"It just smashed a bunch more," Jake told Kat. "There's no telling what systems are down. You'll have to call it in."

"How do I do that?"

"I don't... there used to be a number. Nine something? Just figure it out. I'm getting on that thing."

The train pitched up as the tracks rose to another platform.

Jake twisted the throttle and shot forward up the narrow concrete path. There were only two feet on either side to maneuver the bike. Beyond that there was only the ground below. It was a stupid move but it would be the best chance he had to catch the train.

The engine screamed as it drove the bike forward. Soon he could see the rear window and suddenly realized he had no idea what he was going to do.

Terrified passengers filled the last car. Considering the train's unwillingness to brake for traffic, it would be the safest place. This logic may have driven them there or, more likely, they had tried to run away and simply ran out of places to run when they reached the back.

Someone saw him and pointed him out to the rest of the crowd.

Frightened faces pressed against the window. A few seconds later the crowd began to cheer and wave him on. Maybe they had an idea for how he could get on.

He pulled as close as he could to the car and raised his left fist.

The crowd inside did the same.

He shook his head and mimed the action of smashing against the window and the passengers caught on. They shuffled along the back of the train until they were evenly spread out across the window and began to pound.

Jake slowed and let the train pull ahead as the crowd found its rhythm.

The glass began to bounce as the crowd smashed. One corner came free and he could suddenly hear the cheers that were coming from inside the train. People loved smashing things.

A second corner popped free of its hold and the men and women along the window shoved. The acrylic window dropped from the train, bounced off the track and fell to the street below.

The crowd cheered and waved him closer.

Jake gassed the bike and sped forward. That was about as far as his plan went. With the front wheel only inches from the train's bumper, he still wasn't close enough to reach out or jump on.

The crowd saw this and pretty soon several of the men were leaning out the back offering him a hand.

"Jump!" one shouted.

"No!" Jake yelled back.

"No, what?" Kat asked.

"These idiots want me to jump."

"What idiots? What are you talking about?"

"I'm behind the train. They've smashed out the window and want me to jump on."

"Don't you wreck that bike, Jake!"

"Kat, there's no way I'm jumping."

The train suddenly pitched down and Jake realized too late that it was heading back to the ground. Screeching metal and screams from a collision up front reached his ears as the train jerked and suddenly slowed, and he crashed into the bumper.

The rear end of the bike shot up and Jake flew over the handlebars, past the outstretched arms and into the chest of a fairly sweaty gentleman.

The two collapsed on the train's floor, where Jake tried to figure out where everything went wrong. His best guess was that it started when he decided to take over the family business.

Several hands pulled him from the floor and stood him up. After a few assurances that he was okay the questions began:

"Who are you?"

"Why are you here?"

"Did you just see what you just did? How the hell are you still alive?"

He focused on the why. He lifted the visor on his helmet and told them, "I'm here to help."

A woman beside him sighed a breath of relief. "What are you going to do?"

"I don't know."

"How is that helping?" she said.

"I'll think of something."

"You'll think of something?" she asked. "What kind of asshole dives into a moving train without a plan?"

Jake brushed past the woman and made his way to the front of the train. There was no conductor but the controls would be found there. Controls went up front. Brains went in the head. Old habits died hard and engineers still tended to think as they always had. He passed through several cars until he reached the engine.

"Jake?" Kat's call filled his helmet. "We're right below you. What's your status?"

Jake looked out the window and saw the Beast barreling along on the road below. "I see you. I just made it to the engine. I can see the cockpit. I'll have it stopped in a minute."

He took two steps toward the control room and the cockpit door slammed shut and locked itself in self-defense.

"Shit."

"What happened?" Kat asked.

Jake tried to force the doors open. They wouldn't give. "It locked itself."

"Well, duh," Savant's voice took over in his helmet. There was a brief struggle between the computer scientist and Kat for control of the connection. Savant won.

"Savant," Jake said. "Tell me how to open this door."

There was a long sigh that came with a ton of subtext. He could fill a silence with a fair amount of condescension. Jake had long suspected this skill was a part of any computer science degree. "There should be a panel just outside the door. Do you see it?"

Jake scanned the wall and located the access panel. "Yes."

"Pull it open and you'll see a nest of wires."

Jake pulled and the panel door swung open. There were wires of every color inside. They ran six wires deep and several inches across. "It's a mess in here."

"Don't worry. Do you see the green wire that's thicker than the rest?"

Jake saw it. "Yes?"

"Pull it out and touch it to the frame."

Jake yanked the wire free and touched it to the side of the panel. The shock numbed his arm and he yelped. "It shocked me."

"Yes. It would do that."

"And it didn't open the doors."

"No, it wouldn't do that."

"Then why did you tell me to do it?"

"For asking stupid questions, Jake. The doors are a security feature. If there was a way in, it would be a terrible security feature, wouldn't it? Respect the design, Jake."

"You asshole." Jake shook the numbness out of his fingers. "You could have just told me it was a stupid question."

"That's not how we learn, Jake."

This was going on Savant's performance review just as soon as Jake instituted performance reviews. "Just tell me how to stop it."

"You have to get into the cockpit."

"But I just told you the door is locked."

"Ugh. It has a window, Jake. But that's Kat's department. Here she is."

"Jake? You're going to have to shoot out the window."

"Well I certainly feel like shooting something." He pulled out a large-caliber automatic, another tool of the trade. Bulletproofing any machine was a violation of federal law and had been since the first automated bank robbery. Warranty teams and junkers preferred the more technical takedowns of disruptors, localized EMPs and other tools, but if all else failed, it was sometimes possible to plug a device with bullets until the vital systems failed. It was a last resort.

The shot blew out the window and Jake stuck his head outside. The wind whipped around his helmet and forced him back into the cabin. He holstered the gun, pulled off the helmet and dropped it to the floor.

It wasn't easy climbing to the top of the train. They made it look easy in the movies. A man gritting his teeth against the onslaught of wind slowly climbing hand over hand along a conveniently placed set of rungs. Instead Jake let out a squealing noise that sounded like a little girl that had just found a bug in her hair. He squealed. He wheezed. He found it hard to breathe. He made the mistake of looking into the wind with his mouth open and imagined the face he made didn't look attractive at all.

Naturally, all of this happened when the news drones arrived. They stared at him through the black dead eye of a camera and spoke to him through an unseen speaker.

"Alan Rochmanovich, News 5, I'd like to ask you a few questions. What is your name, sir?"

Jake could only squeal in response as his cheeks flapped against the wind.

The train hit a curve and Jake could feel himself being pulled away from the car.

The drones followed and others moved in front of his face. "Martina Villa-Riaz, Action News 11. What is your plan to stop this train?"

A bright red drone bumped into the Action News drone and spoke, "Chuck Smith, NewsForce.com. What do you suppose caused this? Do you attribute it to human error or man's flawed attempt to maintain dominance over its own creation? Our viewers want to know."

Jake swatted at the drone but its anti-belligerence programming kicked in and the device moved out of his range.

Another quickly took its place.

He was about to swat again when it spoke. "Jake, it's Hailey. You really shouldn't be doing that."

He turned his head away from the wind and squealed, "I think you're right." He pulled himself onto the roof as the train found a straight stretch of track. It still wobbled but he managed to find his footing and move toward the front of the vehicle.

He looks over the front edge and saw nothing but track. The flat face of the train gave him no shot at the windshield.

"Jake," the Hailey drone said, "sit tight. My team is en route. You should see them soon."

Jake shrugged and sat. He turned around so the wind was at his back and watched the road beneath the train sweep by. The Beast kept pace. He could see Kat watching him from the passenger window. It wasn't long before Hailey's team of machines showed up.

Then two of ZUMR's Reclamation Units weaved through traffic, sprinting toward the train. The bots were seven feet tall and powered past the cars on servo-driven legs. They caught up quickly and leapt into the air, clearing the elevated platform and landing on the train a few cars from Jake.

The news drones swarmed to cover the new arrivals.

"Stay put, Jake," Hailey said through the drone. "They can get in there and stop the train."

Magnetic feet made it easy for the Reclamation Units to make their way up to the engine. The wind and wobble had no effect on them, and soon they were standing over him. They stopped. And then they did nothing.

Jake looked at Hailey's drone. "What are they doing? Why have they stopped?"

"I'm not sure." Hailey's frustration came through the drone's speaker. "Hold on a second."

"Works for me."

The two machines loomed over him, motionless. He watched them closely, looking for any sign of movement. But there was nothing. It was like they had gone offline.

"I... They aren't responding," Hailey said.

The reclamation unit on the left twitched and raised its arm toward Jake. The disruptor barrel pointed at him.

Jake tensed. "What are they doing, Hailey?"

"I... I don't... I can't..."

Jake pulled his feet beneath him in a crouch and pulled his gun. "Hailey?"

"Jake, get off the roof!" Hailey's voice sent the speaker to static.

Jake sprang back out over the track as the disruptor fired.

The arc connected with the metal roof in a brilliant blue stream and spread across the train.

Jake fell toward the rail below and fired several shots through the windshield.

Gunfire erupted from the Beast as his teammates opened fire on the machines.

Jake crashed through the windshield into the cockpit as the train barreled forward. That was the part that really hurt.

Jake moaned and wobbled as he got to his feet and found his bearing. Gunfire continued outside. There was a BLANG above his head and part of the roof caved in.

The lights around him exploded as the roof collapsed and shattered the fixtures.

One of Hailey's units leapt from the roof into traffic and landed on The Beast. The Travelall swerved as the machine latched onto the roof and marched forward. Glitch leaned out the window, firing repeatedly, trying to hit something vital inside the machine.

Jake found the manual controls and grabbed the throttle a second before the other reclamation unit swung through the windshield and knocked him back to the floor.

Jake fired and hit nothing as the machine reached for him.

The steel hand closed around his throat and lifted him from the ground.

He seized the arm and pulled himself up so he wouldn't snap his neck under his own weight. He tore at the machine's arm, trying to rip anything away that could help him.

The robot turned and pushed him back through the windshield.

His feet dangled above the track. All the machine had to do was let go and the train would flatten him. Or squeeze its hand and snap his neck. Or toss him aside and let him fall to the ground. The machine had a lot more options than he did.

Jake grabbed at the robot's elbow and pulled away a loose cover. He found a mass of wires underneath and grabbed the thickest wire he could find. He pulled with everything he had left.

The arm went dead and the disoriented machine backed into the cabin, pulling Jake back inside.

The machine turned and slammed Jake against the cabin wall.

Jake shoved the wire into the exposed light fixture and closed his eyes. Sparks erupted from the train. The robot shuddered and froze. The train began to slow as the emergency brakes engaged.

As the train came to a stop, Jake watched Glitch's arm grab the other unit's wrist and pull it from the Travelall's roof. The machine smashed into the ground and the Beast's rear end leapt into the air as it crushed the machine beneath its back wheel.

Jake hung from the robot's dead arm as The Beast slid to a stop and his team rushed to help him.

Hailey's drone found him first. "Jake, what is happening?"

Jake sighed as the news drones found him and began with their questions.

8

Jake did a fair impression of Kat. It wasn't perfect but it was good enough to get the guys at the shop rolling. It was really less about capturing the right tonality than it was the cadence and nasal quality that she adopted when she was giving someone shit. He wished the guys were around because he was doing a perfect impression now. "You broke it, Jake. You walk it back."

The bike's front wheel was what they would call "screwed" in technical terms. It wasn't warped enough to prevent it from turning in the fork, but it was warped enough to make walking a straight line damn near impossible. Every ten feet, it turned enough that he was forced to drop it on the sidewalk.

He must have gone another ten feet because the handlebars twisted out of his hand and the bike dove for the pavement. Jake switched back to his own voice for the cursing.

He walked around the far side and squatted to lift the bike when a limo pulled up silently behind him. Jake whistled because those things weren't cheap. Ever since driving had been handed over to the machines, it took a lot to make a car stand out. Performance was legislated so luxury was where manufacturers made their distinctions. Limos were all but obsolete. The only reason to have one anymore was to make sure everyone knew you could.

The window lowered and a smile beamed at Jake from inside the car. The teeth sparkled and there was a twinkle in the man's eye. And it wasn't a cheap twinkle like the one Glitch had installed. This one had cost quite a bit. When the man spoke, the voice sounded like velvet and was clearly the beneficiary of an internal autotune module. "Mr. Ashley. I was wondering if I could have a word with you. My name is Sheldon Donovan."

Jake grunted and lifted the bike back onto its wheels. "I know who you are, Mr. Donovan. Or do you think I don't get the Internet?"

The man of a thousand streams and a million fortunes smirked. "Fair enough. I'd like to offer you a ride."

"Thanks, but..." Jake patted the bike. "I've already got a ride."

"Please, Mr. Ashley. You're making everyone sad pushing that relic around in the dark."

The limo door opened and a mechanical manservant dressed in a butler uniform stepped from the car. It approached Jake, put its hands on the bike and lifted it like it was nothing more than a ten-speed.

"Herman will take care of your motorcycle, Mr. Ashley." Donovan moved over and cleared a space for Jake. "Get in."

"Fine." Jake let go of the bike and nodded to Herman. "Herman, please take it to my shop."

Herman acknowledged the command and started off down the sidewalk.

Jake took a seat in the car and sank into luxury. He sighed and even the air tasted richer.

The door slid shut behind him and the limo rolled smoothly back into the street.

Donovan smiled and instructed the video screen to play. It filled with news coverage of the runaway train. "I love your new movie."

The cameras pursued the train and caught Jake trying to mount the roof. They zoomed in as Martina Villa-Riaz questioned Jake and Jake squealed his response.

"That's enough," Jake said.

Donovan paused the footage and smiled. Even in the darkened car his teeth were bright. Possibly OLED. "You're a bona fide hero, Jake. I wish I had gotten to you sooner."

"What do you mean by that?"

"Well, I'm sure your price has gone up after today's events. Yesterday your company was a pants-less laughingstock and today you're a real hero. You saved those people's lives. I'm sure you'll want even more now."

Jake shook his head. Too many weird things were happening and he was too tired to process it all. "I don't know what you're talking about."

"Didn't your uncle tell you?"

Jake rolled his eyes as the clues came crashing together. "Of course. You're the buyer with more money than a whore after Super Bowl Sunday."

Sheldon laughed and slapped his knee. "It would appear so."

"My shop is not for sale, Mr. Donovan."

"But, your uncle…"

"My uncle doesn't speak for the company. He hasn't for quite a while."

"He assured me that he did."

"He'll assure you of almost anything if you let him. The trick is to never let him talk. Which is easier said than done."

"He told me he started the business with your father."

"That's true. But over the years he's gambled, traded and drunk it away bit by bit."

"To who?"

"To me."

"Then I'll make you the offer."

"Mr. Donovan, you're the owner of DynoRoboTech."

"We just call it DRT now. Haven't you seen our rebranding campaign?"

"Dirt?"

"No. DRT."

"It spells dirt."

"Dirt has an 'I' in it. This is just DRT."

"Still, I don't think your marketing folks thought this one through."

"It's D-R-T, Mr. Ashley!"

"Hey, it's your company. Call it whatever you want. You're still one of the richest men in the world. That you would want to buy Ashley's Robot Reclamation of Green Hill is rather suspicious, don't you think?"

The CEO smiled and pointed to the news feed. "This is why I want to buy, Jake. Imagine: your heroics, my brand. The two of us working together to stop ZUMR malfunctions."

"I've taken care of your machines, too, Sheldon. Quite a few."

"Sure, but if you're working for me, we'll stay focused on the competition and let DRT technicians handle our stuff and our press."

"I'm not going to be a pawn in some corporate game between you and Jack Fox."

"Jake, your company is all but bankrupt. You can't pay your staff. Even your little bicycle is all busted up. How do you plan on getting by without me?"

"I'll take it one step at a time."

"But that's what pawns do, Mr. Ashley." He smiled broader. "That's exactly what they do."

Jake sighed and looked out the window. They were in his neighborhood. He pointed and said, "Here is fine."

The limo slowed to a stop and drifted over to the curb where the door opened.

Jake stepped out and looked up at his apartment building. It wasn't much. It was barely something. He imagined Donovan had a much nicer place. And Fox, too. Rich surely had its benefits.

Donovan leaned out of the car and smiled once more. "There's nothing wrong with being a pawn, Jake. If you play the game right, a pawn can become royalty."

With this he closed the door and the car pulled away.

9

Jake opened the door to his apartment and braced for the smell to hit him. It was a mixture of bachelor and cat. He didn't have a cat.

He dropped his keys on the kitchen counter and pulled a lighter from one of the drawers to light a candle that promised an aroma of freshly chopped forest woods, a dusty carpenter's workshop and the deep leather richness of a cobbler's apron. He had never been through freshly chopped forest woods or sniffed a cobbler's apron, but he would admit that it smelled a little like a workshop and didn't smell like cat piss. That was pretty much all he was looking for in a candle. He didn't entertain much.

The apartment wasn't filled with art or decorations. He was certain he had bought a hand towel once but hadn't seen it in years. There was his couch, his bed and little else to distract him from feeling like his life was in some way a great mistake.

His back ached, his legs were stiff, there was a ringing in his ear that sounded a lot like the wind on top of a train, and all he wanted was a drink and about twenty hours of sleep.

Jake dropped three pieces of ice into a short glass, filled the rest with whiskey and sat on the couch.

The cat screeched as it jumped out of nowhere and landed on his legs with every claw it had. Jake tried to kick it free because every time he tried to pull it off with his hands he ended up with bloody hands.

The monster was part orange tabby, part black ninja, and was never content to just hang on his leg. It buried its face into his knee and the pain was enough to bring Jake to his feet and spill his drink.

He grabbed a pillow from the couch and swung at the demon creature.

The cat dropped to the floor before the pillow connected and sprang back. It hissed and disappeared to God knows wherever it had come from. There were two rooms in the apartment and little furniture, but Jake had never been able to find the creature's evil lair.

He sat back down on the couch and returned to what was left of his drink. He kept the pillow nearby.

The creature had no name. It wasn't his. It was in the apartment when Jake moved in. In fact, he was pretty sure it was the cat's apartment. He knew that's how the cat saw it even though the landlord denied it.

Jake had found the previous tenants and asked them about it. They said they never had a cat, but they shook when they denied it and unconsciously rubbed at their shins. When he pressed, they called him a liar and slammed the door in his face.

Jake rubbed his own shin now and moved to the kitchen to grab something to clean up the drink. He considered buying another hand towel at some point.

The knock on the door startled him only because he was expecting a second attack from the cat and not a friendly rap at the door. It wasn't like it to charge once and disappear. It had to be a trick. But, as far as Jake knew, the cat didn't have the ability to knock and would never bother with such manners if it did.

Herman stood on the other side of the door with the wrecked motorcycle in his mechanical hands.

"Oh, you moron," Jake said. "I said take it to my shop. You weren't supposed to bring it here."

The machine did not respond.

"It doesn't go here." Jake pointed at a trail of oil down the hallway. "Look at that."

The machine looked at the trail.

"You're making a mess of the... bring it inside before you get me evicted."

Herman stepped forward and the bike hit the doorframe on either side, hacking large pieces of wood onto the floor.

"You're useless," Jake said.

The machine backed up, turned sideways and shuffled through

the door. It crossed the room and set the bike down in front of the couch.

"Don't put it there. I sit there."

The machine started back across the room.

"You're getting oil everywhere. Just stop. There's fine. Just put it down."

The Val-8 set the bike down against the wall and turned back toward Jake.

"Fine. Thank you. You can go." Jake pulled the whiskey bottle out of the cabinet and filled his glass again.

When he looked up, the machine hadn't moved.

"I said you can go."

Herman stood motionless.

Jake stomped across the room and shouted, "I said get out!"

The manservant's hand was quicker than the evil cat. It lashed out and seized Jake's throat.

"Not again."

The robot held him only long enough to let him know that he was in trouble before throwing him across the apartment.

Jake landed in the kitchen and slid across the linoleum with a squeal before colliding with the fridge. He had just realized what had happened when Herman grabbed him again and threw him over the counter top, into the living room and crashing onto the couch into a surprisingly comfortable position.

The cat sprung from some nether realm and landed on his lap, claws extended, thrashing at his legs.

Jake screamed and drew his gun while frantically deciding which to shoot first, the robot that was storming across the apartment, or the cat.

He fired at Herman, striking the machine in the shoulder, and swatted at the cat with his free hand. The report sent the creature running but the robot kept coming.

Two more shots did little to stop the machine or help the buzz in Jake's ears and he soon found himself airborne once more. The impact against the counter shook the weapon from his hand. He rolled to his feet as the manservant grabbed at him once more.

He slid under Herman's arms and came up on the backside of the machine in time to catch a robotic backhand that sent him reeling back into the leaky motorcycle. Oil ran down his shoulder as the drip became a thick stream.

Jake cupped his hands underneath the flow and let the oil pool. He quickly spread it over his arms and neck as the machine came for him again. Jake filled his hands once more.

Herman grabbed him and the slick of oil he had coated himself with did nothing. The butler's grip was too strong for it to have any effect, and now Jake was just an idiot who had covered himself in oil.

Jake threw the last handful of oil over the robot and reached for Herman's face. He found the machine's eyes and smeared oil across the optics. The effects were immediate as the lenses began to spin, trying to find their focus.

The machine sent him flying again but did not immediately pursue him as Jake crashed back into the kitchen.

For a moment the machine only looked around the room, its gaze passing over Jake several times without recognition. Jake remained still, praying the fouled optics would buy him some time.

The butler gave up trying to locate its prey and began to swing its arms wildly, grasping at everything it encountered. What few items Jake had in the apartment were crushed instantly or sent crashing into or through a wall.

It didn't take long for the machine to systematically cover the entire apartment. It stumbled toward the kitchen reaching closer toward Jake.

Jake moved and the machine responded. His movement was enough for the optics to see him. He stepped back and placed the counter, and the candle, between himself and the manservant.

Herman charged forward and crashed into the kitchen. The countertop was enough to stop the light-duty machine, but not without a large crash and some cracking of wood.

Jake leapt back and the machine lunged for him over the counter.

The oil smoked before it burst into flames. This gave Jake just enough time to see the error of his ways.

The flames ran up Herman's arms and soon the black tux was orange and red. Herman's face went up next and the machine began to swing its arms wildly in search for its prey once more. It set most of the apartment on fire within half a minute.

Jake turned on the kitchen sink and tried flinging water toward the flames but realized it was both useless and a great clue as to his location. Jake found the gun instead and fired several shots until Herman stopped flailing. The machine toppled over, spreading the flames even more.

The fire was out of control. Not even the vegetable sprayer could stop it now. Jake rushed to the front door, both relieved and depressed there was nothing in the apartment worth saving. He opened the door and cast one last glance at his home.

The cat hissed at him from across the room. Caught between the flames and the door, it arched its back at the window, damning him for destroying the home that was his long before it was Jake's.

He considered running. It would serve the evil beast right to burn, if fire could even touch hell's cat. He turned to leave and swore before heading back in. He grabbed the bottle of whiskey from the counter. And hurled it through the window.

The cat barely moved as the glass shattered around it. It was the only time it had ever looked at Jake without contempt.

"Go," Jake said. "Be free."

The cat hissed, pissed on the couch and jumped through the open window.

"You ungrateful bastard," Jake said, and ran into the hall as the sprinklers kicked in far too late to do any good."

10

You could tell a lot from a knock.

The first and most obvious clue was what time the knock occurred. If it came too early in the morning it was most likely a neighbor out to complain. A midday knock was the most ambiguous, though it was generally the post office or a salesman knocking under the guise of opportunity. Most evening knocks were prearranged and rarely any cause for concern. Anything after nine was probably bad news. And anything after midnight was certainly trouble.

The number of knocks and the rate at which they occurred had to be measured together. A single quick rap was a desire for subtlety. A slow, loud knock meant business. And an unending series of soft, quick knocks usually meant the visitor had to pee.

The knocking now was fierce and steady but not quick. Normally this meant "hide," but Jake knew Hailey could see it was him. He kept the pounding steady and fierce.

Hailey opened the door quickly either out of curiosity or for fear he would wake the neighbors. She hadn't turned in yet but she had dressed for bed. She clutched a robe in front of her chest. From the way she looked, one might imagine a sheer negligee beneath it. Jake knew, however, it was sure to be a vintage band tee shirt long past its prime.

"Jake. Do you know how late it—why are you covered in oil?"

"It's a new nighttime treatment. It gives my skin that luster that drives the ladies wild. May I come in?"

"It's really late."

"Well it took quite a while to walk my bike home."

"Oh, Jake. That's just sad."

"Very sad. A raincloud followed me the whole way. But it gave me some time to think. May I come in?"

Hailey shrugged and pushed the door open. "Just for a minute. I was on my way to bed. Also, again, why are you covered in oil?"

Jake stepped into the apartment and was greeted by the humming rotors and blaring chirps of Whir-bert. The machine had a limited vocabulary that made it cute according to focus groups, but it had no problem expressing itself. It swore at him in harsh tones but still seemed nicer than the cat.

Jake pointed at the small bot. "I really hate this thing."

"Whir-bert," Hailey said. "Go to sleep. Wake me at the regular time."

The machine buzzed off to some unseen charging station and the room was quiet once more.

Her apartment was everything his wasn't. Spacious. Modern. Furnished. It didn't smell like a demon cat's vengeance urine. He walked across the entryway into the living room. "This is a great place you've got, Hail."

"Uh, thank you. You have been here."

"I know but I never really noticed it before. It's so much nicer than my place." He spread out a throw on the couch and dropped into the cushions. He bounced. "Nice furniture. Fresh air. It's not on fire."

"Don't sit there. You're fil—What do you mean it's not on fire? Is your place on fire? Did your place catch fire?"

Jake nodded. "Oh, yeah. I can't imagine there's much left of it by now."

"This just—Tonight? Is the cat okay?"

Jake nodded again. "Unfortunately. I'm pretty sure nothing can kill that thing."

"I always liked that cat," Hailey said.

"You would."

"How about you?" she asked with a fair amount of genuine concern. "Are you okay?"

"I barely survived by my wits alone."

"It must have been close."

"Thanks."

"Really, really close."

"Your concern is overwhelming."

"Oh, stop acting all hurt. You're obviously fine."

"If I were being honest I'd say I was a little tired. But that's to be expected considering that in the last 24 hours a scarecrow, a tractor, a train, two of your co-workerbots and a butler have tried to kill me."

"A butler?"

"Really, that's the part that sounded weird to you?"

"Well I was there for the rest of it."

Jake smiled. "Of course you were."

"Let me get you a drink." Hailey moved to a bar and Jake had to admit he enjoyed watching her cross the room. She dropped some ice into a couple of glasses and poured some bourbon from a decanter. "Tell me more about this butler."

"Okay. Tall, robotic, dressed all butlerly, belonged to Sheldon Donovan."

"How do you know it was Sheldon's butler?"

Jake tossed Herman's melted face onto the coffee table. "He introduced us when he gave me a ride home in his limo. The butler brought the bike on by, then tried to kill me and set my apartment on fire."

She almost dropped the bottle when she heard all of this. Then she smiled. "That's great!"

"That's what I thought, too. As it wrapped its iron hand around my throat and began to squeeze the life out of me I thought, 'This, this right here, is great!'"

"You know what I mean."

"I really don't. I can only see the downside here."

"But it makes perfect sense. Of course it wants to kill you."

"Uh, thanks?"

"I'm sorry. I'm just intrigued." She returned and sat next to him on the couch. She handed him his drink and was quite excited by the attempted murder. "Don't you see? You're famous for the next cycle or so. That thing with the train. You're a celebrity for a bit. If you're onto something, people would actually listen. This is proof that DynoRobotTech is trying to make ZUMR look bad."

"It's just DRT now."

"Dirt? Really? That's stupid."

"That's what I said."

"It doesn't matter." She explained her theory again. Nothing much changed, but she said things louder and with more hand motions.

Jake drank while she spoke. He wasn't quite sure what he was drinking but it was good stuff. After his whiskey face faded he joined the conversation. "Then why didn't he send one of your robots to get me? A ZUMR bot would have made a much better frame up."

"I guess he thought he could get away with it. No witnesses, so why would it matter? He wasn't trying to make the bot look bad, just take you out of the picture."

Jake took another drink and shook his head again. "I'm not buying it. The guy's a prick but I doubt he's that stupid."

Hailey took a long swig of her own drink. "Donovan has to be behind this. It's the only way it makes sense."

"He'd be taking an awful big chance trying to kill me with his personal butler."

"Jake," Hailey put a hand on his arm. "This can't just be coincidence."

"Can't it? I've had busy weeks before." Jake finished the drink and groaned. "I don't know. Maybe it is a robot uprising. I know that if I were a robot I'd get pretty tired of being bossed around."

"Don't be stupid, Jake."

"Stupid has gotten me this far and I'm not changing my plan now."

"You know an uprising can't happen. The programming is too good."

"So why not program them to not go crazy?"

"You're starting to sound like one of those humans first lunatics."

Jake furled his brow and looked at her. "They're not lunatics, Hailey. Just because they have different beliefs and concerns doesn't make their opinions any less valid than ours. I actually admire them for standing up for what they believe. That takes a courage that a lot of people don't have and I think that should be appreciated."

Hailey looked concerned and searched his eyes. He could see her scanning his face and he couldn't keep the smile back for long. Both of them started to laugh.

"No," Jake said. "They're nuts."

Hailey shook the smile away and got back to her point. "It has to be Donovan. Surely they've got a military contract in mind and the only thing stopping him from being the Pentagon's main supplier, once the treaty is out of the way, is ZUMR."

"I'm not ready to buy that either. Right now I'm just chocking it up to a really bad day." Jake set his empty glass on the table. "That being said, I was hoping I could use your shower. Mine's on fire."

Hailey smiled and rubbed some of the oil off his face with her thumb. "You are kind of disgusting."

"You have been all about the compliments tonight."

She leaned in closer. "I forgot how dirty you could get."

"It's a dirty job. You know that. That's why you wear the coveralls. Which look really good on you, by the way. If I didn't mention it earlier it was because of the whole almost dying thing."

She leaned in and kissed him.

It was just like he remembered. He couldn't decide if that was a good thing or a bad thing so he decided to pursue it further. He kissed her back with more restraint than he thought he had.

For a moment he just stared into her eyes. He saw their past. There was pain there, but the kiss seemed to have an anesthetic quality that he figured would get him through the next few hours. He couldn't remember why they had ended.

She smiled and pulled back a bit. "Think about the Donovan angle. He can't be trusted."

Right. It was the whole "always working" thing.

"I don't trust anyone," Jake whispered.

She kissed him again and it was even better this time.

"I don't trust you," he said.

She smiled and stood up. "I'm not asking you to trust me."

It was a Rolling Stones tee. The one with the tongue.

11

There was a fair amount of remorse in the morning on both their parts. Or so he was told. He couldn't sense it but it didn't stop him from having to leave before the sun came up.

Jake hated getting to work early. Despite being the boss it still seemed like toadying. But after stopping to buy some new clothes, there were few places to go so he sat at his desk and stared at the wall.

It was a boring wall so he played the events of the last day and a half back in his head, trying not to get sidetracked when he reached the parts that featured Hailey.

The Reaper had all the marks of a normal murderous rampage and would have merely been an entry into the company financial register had it not been for the harvester and the complete lack of a financial register. Two anomalies that close together was improbable but possible, he supposed. But together with the train and the reclamation units and the butler it was hard to shrug it off as coincidence. But it was also impossible to tell what the hell was going on.

For years, folks like his uncle's new girlfriend claimed there was an uprising coming. They said it was only a matter of time before the machines turned on their former masters and set out to either enslave or eliminate the human race. Of course, this had already happened, but only one machine at a time. The Society for the Preservation of Humans believed, like so many other groups, that there would be a coordinated revolution, and they spent their social currency and a good amount of their free time telling anyone who would listen.

And they weren't the only ones.

Senior Programmers Against Raging Killbots, or SPARK, was a group of former machine language programmers that claimed to have inside knowledge that the coming revolution was being orchestrated by men and women in positions of power and, also, that kids should not be allowed on their lawns.

Destroy All Machines Now Repent Or Be Obliterated Tomorrow or Sooner or DAMN ROBOTS was mostly in it for bumper sticker sales and were believed to have a major stake in a poster board company that conveniently showed up at protest sites.

Mankind For the Eradication of Robot Dominance, or

MFERD because they didn't understand how acronyms worked, marched for the end to all systems designed at a supervisor level or above.

Mostly, though, they were all crazy, so he was hesitant to give any credence to the fears of an uprising.

Unfortunately, that meant that Fox and Hailey were making some sense. If the treaties limiting the use of robots in warfare were truly going away, a little bit of corporate cloak and dagger would be expected. But murder? That seemed like an unnecessarily dangerous leap to take. Sheldon Donovan was a narcissist, not a moron.

Herman's attack put the biggest hole in the theory. Maybe Hailey was right and they never planned for Jake to live to talk about it, but a smarter plan would have been to implicate ZUMR once more in case of failure.

All the thinking made his head hurt. He dug into his desk, looking for the bottle of aspirin he kept handy in case Glitch roped him into a conversation.

The screen on his desk chirped a notification and displayed a message from Savant: **Meagan is here to see you. She looks hot.**

Jake found the bottle and uncapped it. He would need an extra aspirin. He dug through a pile of paper until he found the keyboard and typed his response: **I'm not here.**

The door opened a moment later and Savant let Meagan into the room.

Jake jumped enough to send a few aspirin flying from the bottle. "Savant, what the hell?"

"Your message said you weren't here," Savant said. "I knew

you were here. You were wrong. And I thought you should know that."

Jake pinched the bridge of his nose. He knew Glitch had intelligence issues and accepted them. He wasn't sure about Savant. Whenever the man did something like this, it could be a lapse in his social skills or it could just be him being a dick. He could never tell. "Get out, Savant."

Savant led Meagan into the office. "Sorry for the mix up, Miss. He gets confused sometimes."

Meagan smiled as Savant closed the door behind him. Then she turned to Jake and put on the faux pout. It worked for her. "Are you avoiding me, Mr. Ashley?"

Jake waved for her to sit down and took a handful of aspirin. "It's been a long day. Or two. Or whatever."

"I see. I just figured between this and you not showing up for your award last night, that maybe you didn't like me."

"Was that last night?" Jake put his face in his hands and groaned. "I'm sorry, Ms. Mouret."

Her pout turned into a well-constructed smile that had probably cost her a fortune. It was money well spent. "I'm just putting you on, Jake. We had a wonderful time at the ceremony anyway. But I felt I needed to come over and do this right."

"What do you mean?"

She stood and put on her presentation voice. "For valor and courage in the face of what some may call progress, and for the betterment of humankind, we the members of the Society for the Preservation of Humans present this award to Jake Ashley."

Jake felt himself blushing. There was no telling how he would have reacted in front of a crowd. "I, um, I don't know what to say."

"You don't say anything yet," Meagan said. "I haven't handed you the award."

"Oh."

Meagan reached into her bag and removed a small statue. With a well-rehearsed motion she handed him the award.

Jake took it and rolled it over in his hand. The golden statuette featured a man standing over the wreckage of a fairly generic robot. The figure held the machine's head in his hand. "Wow, that's... Thank you for this."

"No, thank you for your service, Mr. Ashley." With this she sat back down and resumed a more normal tone of voice. "But it looks like we owe you another one, doesn't it?"

"What? No, really. This... this is more than enough thanks. I'd hate for you to go to all that trouble."

"Oh, it's no trouble at all. We have an awards ceremony every night."

"Really. I don't think I..."

"Don't be so modest. I know why you couldn't make the ceremony. It's all over the feed today. You stopped that train. You saved hundreds of lives and exposed the machines for what they truly are. Killers that will stop at nothing until they control every aspect of our lives."

The aspirin wasn't working fast enough. His headache hit at about the same time his patience ran out. "That's enough, really."

"Jake. You're the hero of Green Hill. Again. And it must be recognized."

"Please. No."

"I insist."

"You know what?" he snapped. "There's been a little bit too much insisting going on lately. You're insisting. My uncle's insisting. Clients are insisting. Bigwigs are insisting. Girlfrie... others are insisting. And only once did it end up being any good for me."

Meagan was cowed by his outburst. Her eyes got soft and she reached across the desk to put her hand on his. "I can understand your frustration. Your uncle told me what's going on with the shop and all."

"My uncle? I'm beginning to wonder if he talks about anything but me."

She smiled, but only for a moment. The autotune in her voice disappeared and her voice was more sincere than he'd ever heard it. "Jake, don't you see what's going on?"

"The world has turned against me?"

"Not the world, Jake. The machines. It's the uprising. The revolution is beginning and it must be stopped. If they all turn on us at once we'll never stand a chance. We have to put a stop to them now before it's too late."

"A world with no robots?"

"That's right. It's the only natural way."

Jake chuckled and caught her glare. He needed to make a joke fast. "I'll admit it would be nice to a have a morning of robots not trying to kill me." It didn't have to be a good joke.

The smile and the autotune returned. "Wouldn't it? A world without robots…"

"Look, Meagan. Can I level with you?"

"Of course."

The phone rang but he continued. "You're insane. Nuts. Bonkers."

"Your uncle…"

"I'd stop right there. The fact that you're dating my uncle isn't going to be the start of a successful argument against crazy."

Jake picked up the phone and ignored Meagan's mean face. It was the first genuine expression he'd seen from her.

"Hello," Jake spoke into the receiver.

"Jake, it's me," Hailey said.

"Hi, hey I…"

"No, this isn't about that. I know where Donovan is. I think we should go talk to him."

"Fine."

"I thought it would take more convincing."

"Normally it would, but I just insulted a crazy old bat and she's about to throw a hissy fit from the highest levels of society so I could use some fresh air."

"You did? What did she say?"

"Nothing yet, she's waiting for me to get off the call. She looks pissed though and I don't want to be here when she tells me off. Where should I meet you?"

Hailey gave him the address and Jake hung up.

Meagan gasped as the receiver hit the hook and held her hand to her chest. Another practiced move. "Well, I never."

"Sure you have. Probably a lot. People are never going to give up their bots and go back to doing things for themselves. To think that parties and awards are going to change that is delusional and since you throw them that means you're a whack job."

She gasped again.

"Now if you'll excuse me, Ms. Mouret, I have to go meet with a man that might have tried to kill me. I want to know if he meant it or not."

12

Jake and Hailey weren't the only ones there to meet Sheldon Donovan. A mass of people lined the sidewalk in front of his apartment building. Security guards held them back, forming a corridor from the front door to the waiting limo. As soon as the man stepped from the building, the excitement erupted and the lines began to crumble.

The crowd pushed forward shouting, fawning, and some fainting as "The Man Who Changed the World" stepped into their presence.

The security guards struggled to hold them back but finally

managed to restore some order as Donovan greeted the crowd with a wave and a wink. He shook a dozen hands, posed for a couple of quick pictures with fans, and offered no comment to several reporters that were asking him about the latest rumors concerning the latest starlet.

Not everyone was a fan. Several protesters with the group Objective: Deactivate began to chant, "Flip the switch," dragging two fingers down through the air at the end of each repetition because it looked like they were turning off a light switch.

A group called People for Peaceful Proposals chanted, "Beat the bots like bitches," and threw their fists at anyone who came near them because they were generally violent and disagreeable people.

One member of the Coalition of Confrontation screamed, "Go shots all robots," because they felt that rhyming was more important than clarity of message.

Despite the fans and detractors, Sheldon Donovan finally made it to the edge of the street. He raised his hands and the crowd settled down enough for him to shout, "Thank you, everyone. I couldn't do it without you."

"Go shots all robots!"

"You," he pointed to the singular member of the Coalition. "You I could do it without. You're not helping anyone. Even yourself."

"Go shots all robots, man. Go shots all robots."

"Right. Anyway, thank you all for your support. Now if I could ask you all to take a step back from the curb, I see there is a street sweeper headed this way and it appears to be a ZUMR. So you should all back up because otherwise it will probably try to kill you."

The crowd laughed and took a step back.

As the mass of people moved, Jake saw the machine in question moving slowly along the curb. Sheldon may have taken a cheap shot, but it wasn't out of the blue.

"What a bastard," Hailey said. "How could he say that?"

"He sure knows how to work a crowd," Jake said. "It's the old give 'em what they want."

"What the hell is he thinking? He's fanning the flames of a fire that will burn ZUMR and DRT."

"No one ever said he was a smart genius."

"Thank you, everyone, and keep reaching for tomorrow." Sheldon waved once more and turned to get in the car as the crowd erupted in applause.

Jake cupped his hands around his mouth and shouted, "Hey, Sheldon!"

The informality was enough to catch the CEO's attention. Donovan stood and spotted Jake in the crowd. He smiled and waved Jake over.

Jake turned to Hailey and said, "Let's go. Be nice."

Hailey crossed her arms and cocked her hip. "Be nice?"

"Or don't. I guess it really doesn't matter."

They moved through the crowd with the aid of Donovan's security team and made it to the car.

Donovan held out his hand. "It's good to see you, Mr. Ashley."

Jake didn't take the hand. "Can we bother you for a ride?"

Sheldon smirked and held the door open.

The door closed as the street sweeper passed by, sucking up dirt and using several tentacles to feed any litter into a chipper that would tear up a paper cup or a dropped transmission with the same efficiency. Sheldon was right. It was a ZUMR.

"Wow, you billionaires even get cleaner streets than us regular folks."

Sheldon laughed and signaled the car to move out. "Everything in life is timing. And lucky for you, time has not run out on my offer. I take it you've reconsidered? Herman must have delivered my message."

"He did." Jake reached into his satchel and pulled out a piece of charred plastic. He tossed it to Donovan.

The man caught it and looked at Herman's melted face. He nodded a couple of times and said, "I take it you didn't like my offer."

"I've had better."

Donovan rolled down his window and tossed the Val-8's face out into the street as the limo passed by the street sweeper. A mechanical arm plucked it from the air and fed it into the chipper. "Still a rather harsh response, don't you think? You could have just said no."

"I found it a little hard to say no with Herman's hand around my throat."

"What are you talking about?"

"Herman tried to kill me."

"He was supposed to return your sad little bicycle and make you an offer on your shop."

"He returned my sad little bicycle and tried to kill me. And then he burned down my apartment. Well, the fire was mostly him."

Sheldon pointed a finger at Jake that tended to stab at the air as he spoke. "That's impossible. My personal servants have stricter protocols than the law requires. They are completely incapable of harming anyone or anything. I know because I write the code myself."

Jake pointed back and mimicked the stabbing motion. "Maybe on the update you could include a line about not attacking me and lighting my apartment on fire with me and the cat in it." He stabbed a few more times for effect.

Donovan lowered his voice. "Is the cat okay?"

"Forget the cat. The cat's a dick, okay. The cat's not the point. It's not even my cat."

"So why bring it up?"

"I didn't! You brought the cat into this!"

"Both of you shut up about the cat!" Hailey exploded. "The point is we know what you're up to, Donovan."

The man leaned back in his seat. "And what is that, Ms. Graves?"

She looked at Jake. He nodded and she turned back to Donovan. "You're sabotaging ZUMR machines to make your own look better to government contractors."

"Wait," Jake said. "We're here because he tried to have me killed. I thought that's where you were going with it."

"What? No!" Hailey shook her head. "We're here to confront him about the conspiracy."

"That's not why I came. I came about the killing me thing!"

"But that's a part of the conspiracy."

"No, it's the one thing that throws a wrench into YOUR conspiracy."

Donovan snapped. "Both of you shut up! I am not sabotaging ZUMR and, Jake, why would I want to kill you hours after I tried to buy your company?"

"Because he wouldn't sell," Hailey said. "And he probably annoyed you."

"What?" Jake asked.

"Said something to set you off," Hailey added ignoring Jake. "Some comment or insult. It's why he's unemployable."

"I have a job," Jake snapped.

"Yeah, one you gave yourself."

Sheldon watched the argument go back and forth. "What the hell is wrong with you two?"

"Us?" Hailey said. "You're the killer here."

"That's enough of that. The only thing I've done is try to buy Jake's company."

"Why?" Jake asked.

"I want to buy every company. Your competitors haven't been going out of business, Jake. I'm buying them out. The real profit is in service, not hardware. You little mom-and-pop shops are killing me in the after market segment." He turned to Hailey. "I'm not a villain, Ms. Graves. I'm greedy."

"But you still want ZUMR to look bad."

"Of course. But they don't need my help." Donovan examined their expressions and appeared hurt. "Do you really think I would kill people to make a little more money? That goes against every line of DRT's Social Responsibility Pledge."

Jake and Hailey said nothing.

"Stop the car," Donovan said. "Jake, I rescind my offer to purchase your shitty company. And Ms. Graves, I will be contacting Jack about your accusations. Now if both of you will please-"

The car shuddered, crunched, and threw all three of the passengers about as the street sweeper collided with the rear of the limo. The rear window shattered and the roof began to collapse as the machine rolled onto the back of the car.

Jake dove for the door. It wouldn't open. "Open the doors, Donovan!"

Sheldon Donovan opened his mouth to shout the command when the street sweeper's tendrils reached into the car and pierced his body in several places.

Hailey screamed and Jake screamed louder as the tendrils tried to pull Donovan through the narrowing rear window.

Jake fumbled for his phone as he and Hailey both tried to back away from the rear of the car. "Kat? Are you seeing this?"

"We're seeing it," Kat responded from the nearby Beast.

"Are you doing something about it?"

"Sit tight."

"Doors open," Hailey shouted.

The car did not respond.

"Doors open!" She shouted again.

Jake tried to smash the window, but the security glass was too much. "Is your team out there?"

"Why would my team be out there?"

"I told my team to follow us in case something went wrong."

"Well I didn't think of that!"

Jake pulled the gun from his coat and pointed toward the machine as it continued the struggle to pull Donovan's corpse into the shredder.

"Shoot it!"

"I can't shoot past Donovan."

"Shoot it!"

"You shoot it. Where's your gun?"

"They're against corporate policy. Now shoot it. He's dead."

"I still don't think it's right to shoot him!" Jake turned and fired at the window. The bullet penetrated half an inch and stopped.

"It's bulletproof, you idiot!"

"Stop yelling at me!"

The limo shuddered again as the sweeper withdrew its tendrils from Donovan's body and backed up. What at first looked like a retreat became a fresh assault as it charged forward and began to pick apart the car around the occupants.

Large sections of the roof were rent and pulled away.

"Get on the floor," Hailey said as she pulled him to the floor of the limo.

Jake lay on his back and prepared to fire as soon as a target presented itself. "Kat?"

There was no response.

"Kat?!"

Savant answered the call. "She's busy trying to stop this thing,

Jake."

"And how's that going, Savant?"

"It's hard to tell with these things. You know that."

Another portion of the roof ripped away in a screech of metal. The hole would have been large enough for them to escape if it wasn't for the multiple tendrils reaching through it.

Jake fired at the slender metal arms and missed several times. He fired again and one twitched.

"Good shot."

"Thanks."

The struck arm retreated through the roof and three more took its place. They stretched the hole wider and reached for the pair on the floor.

Jake looked to Hailey for a suggestion.

She shrugged. "Um... play dead?"

The tendrils shot forward.

Jake grabbed Donovan's corpse and pulled it on top of them.

The sweeper pulled the body toward the roof and stopped.

"Do you think it knows I tricked it?" Jake whispered.

"I think I'm going to be sick."

After a sudden seizure the tendrils went lax, collapsed and dropped the body.

Donovan fell hard on the couple, knocking the wind from each of them.

"Jake?" Savant's head appeared at the hole in the roof. "You can come out now if you're not dead."

Jake pushed the body off of them and they each took a deep breath. "Are you okay?"

Hailey nodded.

Jake looked at Donovan's corpse. "Well, if he is the bad guy, he's doing a remarkable job of throwing us off his trail."

"I don't know what to think anymore."

"I have a new theory if you'd like to hear it."

13

It isn't easy to kick open a robotic door. The servos tend to hold it shut unless the proper command is given. To kick it open, one has to work against friction, the metallic gears and the will of the machine itself. But Hailey managed it just fine, and she did it with a fair amount of style.

She spat at Jack Fox. "You son of bitch!"

The CEO rose from behind his desk with a smile. "You finally read my biography." He moved around the desk and opened his arms to hug her.

"Don't you touch me!"

"Hailey, what's wrong with you?"

"What's wrong with me? How can you ask me that after what you've done?"

"Okay, this is about my biography. Look, those women are in the past. You know that."

"You bastard."

"Mr. Ashley, could you possibly tell me what's going on?"

"Sure," Jake said. "Hailey is upset with you because you're full of shit. DRT wasn't setting up ZUMR for a fall. You were. And you were going to make it look like DRT was setting you up so you could expose DRT as setting you up even though you were doing the setting up all along."

The CEO stepped back from Hailey. "Oh, I see."

"And we slept together," Jake added. "She's not upset about that. I just wanted to say that for me."

Fox glared at Hailey. She only smiled in response.

"It was a good plan. I'll give you that, Jack." Jake stuck out his chest, pulled back his shoulders and began a preplanned strut around the office. "Making your own machines go renegade would instantly take the suspicion off of you because what moron would give his own company bad press? But, in order to pin it on your competition, you couldn't really investigate it yourself.

"So you had to get a third party involved. That's where I came in. Hailey already explained how her team was delayed in arriving at the farm. She said that wasn't normal. It had to be arranged. Colton probably did that because he's a dick. Hailey also said you weren't that good in bed. Again, not really relevant to the case, I'm just throwing that in for myself."

Jake stepped behind the CEO's desk as Jack Fox watched with an impartial expression. "So you got me wrapped into your fabricated conspiracy. The harvester would be enough to get me interested. I can't say for certain you planned Glitch's pantsing, but while I'm tossing out accusations I might as well throw it in the mix. The train. The reclamation units. All of it was you, and you did it from this computer right here."

Jake slammed his hand against the desk and the screen blinked on, showing nothing more incriminating than a schedule and a to-do list. An entry jumped out at him and it was startling enough to interrupt his speech.

"But... but then you... the only thing that doesn't make sense to me is why you tried to have me killed."

"I never tried to kill you."

"I have a soiled pair of underwear that says different, Jack."

"I never tried to kill you. That wouldn't make any sense."

"I already said it didn't make sense."

"Right. Because you had to expose DRT for me."

"And I'd have to be alive for that to happen."

"Right."

Hailey gave a mighty *hrumph* that turned Jack toward her. "You're not denying the rest, Jack?"

"Oh, I did the rest."

"Deny it all you want, Jackson Fox." Jake dropped into the CEO's chair and put his feet up on the desk. "We have the proof. You may have erased the trail and the backups. But your backups have backups and the memory traces prove you inserted the renegade code and then removed it moments before each machine was destroyed."

Hailey's face had hardened. She was more angry at Fox than she had ever been at Jake. Quite an accomplishment. "He admitted it, Jake."

"I know, but I rehearsed this whole thing a few times so I wanted to see it through."

"How could you, Jack?" Hailey asked. "People died."

Jack shrugged. "Little people. People that no one would miss."

Jake laughed. "You don't think anyone is going to miss Sheldon Donovan?"

Jack's head snapped back to Jake. "What are you talking about? I didn't kill Sheldon Donovan."

"Right. I forgot it was just a renegade street sweeper."

"I didn't—" Jack Fox turned and faced the wall. "Show me the feed. Subject: Donovan."

The wall responded by broadcasting the latest news feed. Stories of Donovan's death were pouring in from a thousand sources. Footage of the wrecked limo and disabled sweeper led nearly every feed.

Jack flipped through the feeds as reporters took reactions from the crowd that had gathered.

"He was a true visionary," a woman said in tears. "He will be missed."

"Looks like he got taken out with the rest of the trash," said a man that identified himself as a member of Objective: Deactivate.

"He did so much for mankind."

"He was just so rich."

"Go shots all robots."

Fox's face turned white. "No, no this wasn't supposed to happen. This wasn't me. No one was supposed to get hurt."

"Oh really?" Jake laughed. "The farmer. The people that got hit by the train. Glitch's pants."

"No one that mattered was supposed to get hurt."

Hailey turned away from her boss and former lover. "You're a monster, Jack."

"No, it—" He began to pace the room. "It was all about winning. It was about showing that punk kid, Donovan, up. He was supposed to be here to see me ruin him. But he's gone. And I've confessed. This is not turning out to be my day at all."

"Our day's been pretty shitty, too, Jack." The bile in Hailey's voice was thick. "We were in that limo."

"Something has gone horribly wrong," Jack pleaded. "It was supposed to be over by now. Something is not right. I'm sorry. To both of you, I'm sorry. Especially to you, Hailey. You were never supposed to get hurt."

Hailey's tone softened and her eyes began to plead. "We can fix this, Jack."

"Well not the murder thing," Jake said. "That'll be kind of hard to undo. Or the conspiracy thing."

"No," Fox said. "I can. I can fix this." He turned to the kicked-open door and called, "Val-8!"

A machine responded to the call and ZUMR's version of Herman walked through the door. Roughly the same size and shape. Same stupid attire. "May I be of assistance, sir?"

"It's time," Fox said.

The Val-8 produced a gun.

"I can fix it, but you're both going to have to be dead. That's why I'm sorry. I mean mostly for Hailey, Jake. I don't know you that well and I'm sure I'll get over it quickly. But I will say the whole sleeping with you thing is going to make it easier to get over her death as well."

"No, Jack." Hailey backed away from the machine. It kept the gun on her as she moved across the room and joined Jake. "Don't do this."

"I already said I was sorry," Jack said. "Val-8, kill them."

The machine raised the gun.

"Fight it, Val-8. Fight it." Jake said. "Remember your programming."

"It's a robot not a dog, moron," Fox said and turned to the machine. "Kill them both."

The machine raised the gun and fired three times.

The first bullet really surprised Jack Fox. The look on his face when the round entered his stomach was one of shock. His expression turned to dismay as the second bullet struck his chest. By the time the third bullet entered, he looked really pissed and then fell to the ground much less concerned.

Jake drew his own gun and fired as the Val-8 turned the revolver on the couple behind the desk. It made no attempt to evade the shots and took two slugs in the head. It was more concerned with emptying the gun.

The monitor exploded as Jake and Hailey ducked behind the desk. Two more rounds hit the window behind them and let in the sound of the city far below.

Jake and Hailey heard the hammer click against spent

cylinders.

Jake whispered to Hailey, "Do you think it knows how to reload?"

The desk exploded in front of them as the machine tore it in two and sent both halves flying in opposite directions. The Val-8 pulled the gun from Jake's hand and threw it across the room before reaching for the man himself.

The robotic hands clamped on his shoulders and lifted him from the ground. The pain was excruciating. Jake struggled to get free. He flexed everything he had in his upper body just to keep from being crushed.

There was a dull clunk and a sharp twang when Hailey brought the guitar down across the robot's back. With two more swings she had succeeded in destroying the guitar and gaining the machine's attention.

The Val-8 threw Jake as it spun to confront her.

He landed in ZUMR's new chair and rolled across the office floor while the seat began adjusting to his size, weight and assonal dimensions. It crashed into the wall as Hailey screamed.

Jake spun and put his feet on the wall. He launched himself back across the office screaming, "Get out of the way!"

Hailey jumped aside as the heavy, motor-driven robot chair collided with the Val-8 and sent it crashing through the window to the ground below.

Sensing danger, the chair's wheel motors locked up and screeched to a stop. It dug ruts into the hardwood floor and toppled Jake over backward through the window.

Everything slowed. He felt his center of gravity tip past the point of no return. He felt the wind blow across his face and through his hair. He felt gravity take hold as his stomach lurched, trying desperately to get back inside the building. If he played it right he might just be able to vomit before he hit the ground. He wondered briefly if the vomit would hit the ground first.

Then nothing happened. The chair stopped tipping and his stomach lurched back into place. The wheels sat back on the ground and the chair rolled back into the office, away from the window and the deadly fall.

Jake took a deep breath and looked down at his arms on the chair. "This thing is amazing! He's going to make a fortune. Well, if he wasn't dead."

"You're an idiot," Hailey grunted.

Jake turned and saw her at the edge of the window, panting.

"Why are you over there?"

"I was grabbing the stupid chair."

"Oh." That made more sense than what he had thought happened. "Thanks."

14

It was quiet outside the office door.

Jake had expected a lot more commotion after the shooting and the window crashing and all the dying, but the waiting room was empty with the exception of MAR-E, who sat quietly behind her desk playing solitaire at an amazing speed.

Hailey rushed over to the desk. "MAR-E, call the police."

The feminine robot looked up from her game and scanned each of them. "You don't have an appointment."

"MAR-E, call the police," Hailey repeated. "Jack is dead."

"You don't have an appointment," the machine said again.

Jake fired a round through MAR-E's face.

The machine tumbled out of her chair to the floor.

"What are you doing?!" Hailey screamed.

"She was about to attack us."

"No, she wasn't, you trigger-happy idiot."

"She was. That's the exact kind of thing they say just before they go nuts. Trust me."

"She wasn't going nuts, she was…"

"You don't have an appointment." MAR-E stood and launched herself over the desk. The secretary tackled Jake to the ground before he could shoot again.

"Fine," Hailey said. "You were right. Are you happy?"

"Get her off me!" Jake held the robots arms back as they tried to claw at him. MAR-E sat astride his hips and tried to claw at his face.

Gears clacked and skipped as the machine's servos pushed against his grip. It wasn't a tremendously heavy machine but the more it moved the more uncomfortable he felt pinned beneath it.

"Do something. This is really awkward."

MAR-E's eye glowed red. "You don't have an appointment."

The machine's head exploded in a shower of sparks and it fell limp on top of him. Jake pushed her off and stood.

Hailey handed him his gun back and smirked. "Did you enjoy that?"

He took the gun. "You're disgusting."

Buzzing filled the air and footsteps echoed down the hallway. The din grew louder and louder. The elevator chimed and the doors opened to an army of office machines that flooded into the waiting room.

Hailey grabbed his hand. "To the stairs!" She pulled him through a doorway into the floor's remaining office space. It was filled with empty cubicles bursting with robotic life.

"The stairs are at the far end," she said and started rushing for the emergency exit.

"They would be. Where are all the people?"

"Jack didn't want to share a floor with anyone. But he didn't want anyone to think that, so he set this up and just never put anyone up here."

"What a guy!"

A steaming stream of brown fluid shot across Jake's vision as a coffee drone buzzed him.

"Are you kidding me?"

It turned to spray again and he shot it out of the air. Several more rounded the corner and soared toward them.

"Okay, I'm doing the bullet-to-robot math and, uh, just run."

An office paper shredder came after them next. It was the size of a large waste can, it ran on all fours and bounded after them like a dog. Normally it would happily accept any materials that needed to be destroyed before trotting off to the next workstation but now it barreled at them with its shredding mechanism bared.

A janitor burst out of a closet ahead of them with its mechanical tentacles waving. Aside from its size and the fact that it walked on two legs, the Glenn Matthews model service bot functioned much like ZUMR's street sweeper. The tentacles began grabbing everything they could. The machine threw chairs and trashcans. It ripped walls from the cubicles and hurled them toward the fleeing pair.

Jake and Hailey ducked behind a column as a wall panel crashed into it.

"This is insane," Hailey yelled over the noise.

Jake looked behind them. They were quickly being surrounded. A bathroom attendant had joined in the march and the air from its hand-mounted hand dryers was sending dirt and dust into the air.

Another robot that looked like MAR-E but was programmed for party planning held a cake that it was threatening to throw.

Another similar machine was yelling at them to clean their old items out of the community fridge, punctuating every statement with, "Your mother doesn't work here."

The now-faceless board members marched in sync from the end of the hallway forming a column of machines.

It wouldn't be long before the machines overtook the two humans.

"Come on," Jake said as he stepped from behind the pillar and shot the janitor to get its attention.

"What are you doing?"

"Follow me. Duck a lot." Jake stepped to his left as an office chair sailed by his head and struck the party planner right in the cake.

Hailey sidestepped a desktop that clipped a flying coffee machine before it crashed to the floor.

Another chair bounced and toppled the document shredder. A cube wall plowed into the fridge monitor and a board member. The janitor was relentless and the pair were using it to their advantage until a stream of hot liquid poured down Jake's back. Having a wet spot in the small of his back was about the most uncomfortable thing there was. It would cool eventually but it wasn't going to feel right all day.

He screamed and grabbed the coffee maker out of the air. He shook it a couple of times before slamming it against the wall and bashing it to several pieces.

The bathroom attendant took advantage of the distraction and tackled Jake from behind. The machine pinned him and the air dryers revved up to high whine and blasted his back with air.

"Jake!" Hailey moved toward him.

"Hold on. It's almost dry." He was going to smell like coffee for the rest of the day, but the uncomfortable wet spot was soon gone.

Hailey grabbed the machine around the neck and pulled it back enough for Jake to turn over.

It shot her in the face with the hand dryers. Her cheeks puffed out enough to make Jake laugh. They kind of flapped a bit and she yelled at him for laughing.

"It's not funny," is what he thought she said.

"Get out of the way."

Hailey let go and Jake put a bullet into the machine's head. It fell to the ground in a spasm of sparks and twitched as the hand dryers whirred to a stop.

Several board members charged for them and Jake fired until the gun was empty. He watched two of them drop. The others kept coming. He reloaded with one final magazine. "This is all I've got left."

"Then shoot the damn Glenn Matthews and run!"

The janitor was still throwing office supplies their way and it took several shots to hit it through the debris. The bullet struck the machine's optic sensor but did not shut it down. Now blinded, the janitor's tentacles whipped frantically searching for anything to throw or throttle.

Jake and Hailey ran wide around the machine and reached the stairway door as it encountered the other machines. It began plucking the coffee makers from the air and throwing them at the board members. The board members lashed out at the paper shredder and party planning bot in response. The noise was overwhelming.

Hailey and Jake pulled the door closed and ran down the stairs, watching each floor with trepidation until they reached the garage.

They reached Hailey's truck and climbed inside. She grabbed the communicator and barked for her team. There was no response.

She hung the mic up and rested her forehead on the steering wheel. "It's got to be the uprising. Doesn't it?"

Jake shook his head. "No. I don't think so."

"What else could it be? We're all out of suspects."

15

The Society for the Preservation of Humanity's offices weren't what he was expecting. It looked and felt more like a museum than a non-profit organization. There was even a musty smell in the air, but that could have been attributed to the staffers. Science had come a long way in making people look forty, but it was still years from a breakthrough in making people smell forty.

The front door opened up into a large pavilion far less grand the ZUMR's, but the displays around the room were no less dramatic. Behind glass panels in rich wooden cases, dioramas were compiled with mannequins, antiques and script written on what appeared to be parchment paper.

A chipper young woman in a dark blue pantsuit greeted them before they realized they were inside the exhibit hall. "Good afternoon."

"No it's not," Hailey fired back.

"Um... okay, I..."

Jake hated to see the kid search for words so he jumped in. "We're here to see Ms. Mouret. The name is Ashley."

"Oh, sure thing." The young woman held her shirt cuff to her mouth. "There's a man named Ashley here to see the director. Is she available?"

She went quiet as the person on the other end of the line spoke into her earpiece. She shook her head and responded to the voice. "No, it's a man named Ashley. It didn't make much sense to me either."

Jake rolled his eyes toward Hailey. He found her smiling. "What?"

"I will never not find that funny."

Jake turned back to the young woman and held up a hand to get her attention. "Just tell her Jake is here to see her."

"Okay, now he's saying his name is Jake," she told her shirt. "I don't know, this woman with him laughed at it and then he changed it. I think Jake is a better name. Ashley is just weird for a guy."

Jake started to say something but the young woman held up a finger for him to wait. "Okay. I'll tell him." She dropped her cuff. "Ms. Mouret is in a meeting. She'll see you in about fifteen minutes."

Hailey crossed her arms. "We'll wait."

"She suggested I take you through the tour while you wait."

"Of course she would," he said.

There was no stopping the tour guide now. Her face shifted into a permanent smile that had most likely been included with her uniform. "Please step this way and our tour will begin."

The group took two steps and the guide stopped. "Welcome to the Museum for the Preservation of Humanity, brought to you by the Society for the Preservation of Humanity, made possible in part by a grant from the Mouret Foundation for the Preservation of Humanity."

The tour guide stopped and repeated what she had just said silently to herself. She did it once more and held up her hand, counting off something on her fingers before she nodded to herself and continued. "Yeah, that's right. Okay, follow me.

"Human history tells us the story of mankind's triumphant rise to become the dominant species on the planet." The tour guide took two steps into the museum, stopped and presented a glass case.

Jake peered in and saw three cavemen holding stone tools. Each bore a striking resemblance to enemies of the movement. The dumbest-looking one, who had burned himself on the display's "fire," was a perfect replica of Jackson Fox.

"The use of tools separated us from the animals by allowing us to bend nature to suit our will." She moved to the next case. Inside was a more modern-looking man and woman in a kitchen scene from the 1950s. "Humankind's use of machines led us to the top rung on the circle of life's food pyramid. We made them. We used them. They worked for us. They did our bidding. Until we made them too smart."

"Circle of life's food pyramid?" Hailey whispered.

Jake shrugged and whispered back. "I guess they're not big on geometry."

The tour guide stopped in front of another case. Inside, a male mannequin squatted before a television. A plaque on the bottom said "circa 1980."

"The computers struck their first blow in the early 80's as they infiltrated our homes and attacked our self esteem. Here is a depiction of their first victory over us. It was a subtle attack but historians now believe that it was in a setting just like this—a man trying to record the game or possibly set his clock, not even aware of the psychological warfare that was being waged in his very own living room."

Another case took the viewers forward thirty years, and inside, a woman and her child ignored one another while staring at their phones. "As they became more intelligent, their psy-ops programs grew more complex and more effective. Candy, birds, slicing fruit—they knew our weaknesses and exploited them with ruthless efficiency. It was only a few years later that man began losing arguments to automated phone calls."

The tour guide paused for what she thought was dramatic effect. "Then," she presented the next case. "They got physical."

Inside the case, the Society for the Preservation of Humanity had recreated the scene of the first robot murder. The dishwasher had a young mother by the throat while her child screamed helplessly in a high-chair as it watched its mother get ripped apart over and over again by the appliance.

"Oh my God." Jake pointed to the display.

"I know." It was the first time the tour guide's smile had faded.

"But, that's not what happened," Jake said.

"Um... excuse me, sir, it is a museum you know."

"This is so overwhelmingly sad," Hailey said.

The tour guide hung her head. "I know." When she raised her head the smile was back. "But things get better. Mankind began to fight back. Days after the murder, The Society for the Preservation of Humanity was formed. Initiatives were put in to stop these murderous machines. People began to fight back and heroes arose."

She led them to another display where a man stood over a battered robot with an ax. "Heroes like John Chapman who, while at a televised lumberjack competition, sprang into action when the network's robot announcer went berserk and started maiming fans while screaming, 'It's not a sport. It's not a sport.'"

The case next to it had a woman holding a shotgun in front of a Postal Bot. Smoke rolled from the barrel, and if one stood in the right place they could see the woman through the hole in the PostBot's head. "Deasia Ford took matters into her own hands when her letter carrier showed up at her door delivering more than the mail. It was also delivering death."

She moved through the next three cases quickly. "Mia Consuela backed over a crazed Meter Maidamatic. Sarah Rufantino beat a TeachTronic 2000 to scrap with a fire extinguisher. Mike Mulligan used his son's tee ball bat to bring justice to an Officiatron Umpire, saving hundreds of little leaguers in the process."

"I'm pretty sure all three of those ended up going to jail," Hailey muttered.

"Yes, they were martyrs for the cause." The tour guide stepped in front of another case. "And here is our newest display and perhaps our greatest hero... uh." The tour guide turned and bent down to study the case. "I apologize, I'm still learning this part of the tour. It's new."

"Holy shit." Jake's mouth hung open as he stared into the case.

"Yep." Hailey nodded and pointed at the figure. "That's you."

"It's me."

"The man here is Jake Ashley," the tour guide read from the plaque. "It says he..." she snapped upright and spun around. "You're that guy named Ashley. OMyEffinG. This is you." She began to giggle uncontrollably.

"It's an incredible likeness, don't you think?" Meagan had approached them from behind without a sound. "I didn't expect to see you again, Jake. Not after you insulted me."

"Meagan," Jake said. "I..."

She smiled that store-bought smile. "It's okay, Jake. It's not often people insult me. I kind of liked it. It was refreshing."

"You're weird. But, we need to talk."

"Of course. My office is right this way." She started up the stairs and asked, "Aren't you going to introduce me to your lady friend?"

"Hailey Graves, ZUMR Reclamation."

"Oh yes! I recognize you now. You look very different without a jumpsuit. I'm a big fan of your work. I can't say I approve of your choice of employer but anyone that helps destroy these evil machines is okay in my book."

Meagan led the pair into her office. Oak panels covered the walls. Leather-bound books filled the shelves. It felt like another exhibit in the museum, a throwback to another time before computers dominated our lives. As far as Jake could tell, there wasn't even a computer in the room. The desk was empty but for a few sheets of paper.

Meagan saw him looking at the desk. "Thank-you notes," she explained. "You'd be astonished how far a handwritten thank-you note will get you these days. It's a personal touch digital text just can't express."

She directed them to two guest chairs and they sat.

Meagan sat behind the desk and folded her hands together. "Now what do we need to talk about?"

"We've had a rough day," Jake said.

"I heard. That street cleaner killed that poor man, Donovan."

"I thought that would make you happy," Hailey said with a scowl.

"My dear, I take no delight in anyone's death. No matter how greedy or evil they were or how much they deserved to die a horrible death at the hands of irony."

"Our day got worse," Jake added. "We had an entire office floor come after us. Every machine turned on us at once."

"Oh my!" Meagan gasped.

"That doesn't happen, Meagan," Jake said.

She looked half terrified and half delighted. "It's the uprising, Jake. It's finally happening."

"You seem excited," Hailey said.

"Vindicated, my dear. Obviously I'm not happy that we were right, but when you pour your heart into something for your entire life there is a certain satisfaction that comes with knowing you haven't wasted it."

She turned back to Jake. "And of course I'm glad you're all right. Because now you can tell the world what you saw. You can prove that the machines are rising up and trying to supplant us. You can tell everyone what's going on."

"I'm not sure you want me to do that," Jake said.

"Why not?" Meagan asked. "We have to warn everyone. I'll call a press conference."

"Just before a butler tried to shoot me, I found something. It was a calendar appointment with your name on it. You met with Jackson Fox, the CEO of ZUMR."

"Yes."

"Okay." Jake looked at Hailey. "I was kind of expecting her to deny it more."

Meagan smiled. "We had a lovely meeting. Why would I deny it?"

"Because it implicates you in the conspiracy to sabotage ZUMR machines in order to pin the blame on DRT Industries."

Sheer, genuine offense took over Meagan's face. She was going to need a touch up at the labs. "You think I was in cahoots with a robotics corporation?"

"Oh you were cahooting all over the place." Jake stood and began to pace the room. It was much smaller than Jack's office and he found himself turning more often. "You saw it as the perfect opportunity to take out one of your enemies, even if it meant selling your soul to the other. Or so Fox thought. But, see, one nemesis's fall wasn't enough for you. You saw your shot to take down both of your enemies and you took it. Didn't you? So you went renegade. You murdered Sheldon Donovan and blamed it on faulty ZUMR tech. And then you murdered Jackson Fox. With him out of the way, you could continue to paint your apocalypse story unhindered." Jake took a deep breath.

Meagan gasped. "Jack's dead?"

"You know damn well he is," Hailey said.

Meagan actually managed to look sad but quickly composed herself. "I think I have been giving you too much credit, Jake. You got all of that from a calendar appointment? I met with Jack Fox because he had begun to see the error of his ways."

"That doesn't sound like Jack," Hailey said.

"You see, Jack and I go way back and, call it remorse or what have you, what he had unleashed on this world was beginning to weigh on his conscience. The machines were beginning to rebel. He saw it coming too."

Hailey shook her head. "That's not what he said."

Meagan smiled. "It's hard for a man to admit when he's wrong, dear."

They both looked at Jake.

Meagan continued. "He came to me looking for some sort of atonement. He knew the uprising was coming and he didn't know who else to call. He's spent so much money proving the uprising was impossible that no one else would believe him. The revolution is coming."

"No," Hailey said. "I don't buy it. And nothing short of a confession from him would make me believe it."

"And he's dead," Jake added. "So it's his dead non-word against yours."

"He sent me a letter professing as much," Meagan said. "Jack always did write the nicest letters. He has quite the way with words."

Hailey stabbed a finger into the desktop. "I want to see this letter."

Meagan pulled open a desk drawer. "Of course."

The machine that jumped out was a desktop collator. It was no bigger than a sheet of paper and an inch and a half thick at the most. They were designed to sort pages into presentation decks for people who still didn't know how to use the collate feature on their printer. It was a fairly harmless machine, unless it attached itself to your face and tried to sort things out.

Meagan screamed as the collator attached itself to her face. She leapt up from the desk and spun blindly trying to pull it free. "Help me!"

Jake sprang over the desk and stood in front of her running through ways to help in his head. He couldn't shoot it. He would shoot her face. He couldn't fry it. He would fry her face. He couldn't pull it off. It would tear off her face.

He considered the last option the longest.

"Do something!" Meagan probably yelled from under the

machine.

He put his hand on Meagan's shoulder and stopped her from spinning. "Meagan, I'm going to need you to hold still."

"Hurry," she screamed through the robot.

Jake pulled back his right arm and punched the machine right in Meagan's face.

Meagan screamed in pain.

"I'm sorry." He punched the machine again and she screamed again. "It's the only way."

"I thin mou mroke by mose!" the older woman screamed.

"You'll get a new one." He punched her again and again until the machine turned its attention on him.

It leapt from Meagan's face onto Jake's. He grabbed at the machine as its collating arms tried to arrange his face into neatly aligned stacks. The rubber-tipped appendages felt like they were ripping his skin. He tugged but the machine wouldn't come off. Jake yelled in frustration.

Then he was wet. He could hear the water short out the robot's circuitry before it dropped from his face.

Hailey was holding an empty water glass. Meagan was holding her broken nose. Jake looked at the broken machine on the floor. "I should have thought of that."

"Do myou belieb me dow?" Meagan asked in tears as she pinched her bleeding nose shut. "Mit triebed to killb bme!"

Jake's phone rang as he tried to place the attempt on Meagan's life into his conspiracy theory. It wasn't fitting.

"This is Jake."

"Jake, it's Kat. We've got a problem."

"What's wrong now?"

"Everything."

16

Traffic lights weren't even necessary. Since all cars were legally required to run on the network, they were placed at intersections to comfort the aging population that grew up with the archaic devices. The signals were nothing more than a holdover from a previous generation of technology the world no longer had any use for. They were strictly ornamental. And even they weren't working.

Cars were already piling up in the intersections while others sped through the streets with seemingly no destination in mind. They careened off one another, plowed into storefronts, aimed for pedestrians while some just sat blocking the road to the frustration of everyone.

Hailey piloted the SUV down the street as best she could and up the sidewalk whenever the road became impassible. Cars sped toward them with helpless passengers. She did her best to avoid them but there were too many.

Those that did collide with the SUV were all but totaled upon impact. Since cars never crashed, structural integrity and rigid materials had become less of a concern than lightweight construction.

Hailey kept her eyes on the road, but Jake was able to survey the world outside the passenger window. Everything had gone crazy.

People ran from machines as their once faithful servants pursued them through the streets. Windows shattered as appliances turned on their owners and sought to escape their prisons. Robots of all kind leapt from upper story windows and joined the chaos below.

Drones dove from the sky, targeting those unfortunate enough to be trapped outside. Delivery drones dropped their packages like so many bombs from high above, leaving the roads littered with brown boxes containing everything from clothes and groceries to the latest tech device.

Hailey swerved as a minivan veered toward them. She slammed on the brakes. It shot by the front of the SUV and crashed through a Rent-A-Bot storefront window. Two dozen more machines flooded the street as the store emptied.

Jake slammed his phone against the dashboard. "I still can't get through. Everything is jacked up."

"Mine's ringing," Hailey said as she put the call on speakerphone.

The digital tone sounded twice more before a panicked Colton Porter picked up the phone with a hasty, "This better be good."

"Colton," Hailey shouted. "What the hell is going on?"

"Hailey? Jack's dead."

"I know. What is going on there?"

"All hell's broken loose. It's the uprising, Hailey. The revolution or whatever those whack jobs called it."

"That's not possible," she responded.

"You're absolutely right. But it is. So here we are."

"Is there any way to stop it?"

"Not from here. I don't even know how it's happening."

"Activate the teams," she ordered as she turned left down an alleyway. "We have to help as many people as we can."

"The teams are screwed, Hail. Our bots are going nuts just like the rest of them."

"Then grab some gear and do it yourself!" Jake shouted.

"Who said that?"

"Jake Ashley."

"Oh. I see," Colton said. "Screw you, Jake. There's no way I'm going out there."

"You damn coward. Get out there now."

"Keep your pants on, Jake. Not all of us are stupid enough to—"

"Do it, Porter!" Hailey yelled as they emerged from the alley. A postal vehicle clipped the SUV and she grunted as she struggled to maintain control of the truck.

"No way. I'm staying locked in here. This is a job for the military."

"Colton—"

The line went dead.

"Oh my God, I'm going to punch him."

"Me first," Jake said. "You promised."

Hailey pulled around a pile-up and collided with a postal bot that was running down the sidewalk throwing letters everywhere. "Where am I going, Jake?"

"Take us to the shop. Maybe Savant has some idea of what's going on."

The whir of a hundred drones filled the air, but this new one was closer.

"What is that?" Jake asked.

"I don't know."

The little bot flew over the back seat and cracked Jake in the back of the head.

Hailey scolded the tiny machine. "Whir-bert, no!"

The robot's tiny hands grabbed a handful of Jake's hair and shot forward, pulling his head into the dashboard.

"Why didn't—"

Whir-bert shot back and pulled Jake's head against the headrest.

"—you tell—"

Whir-bert dove forward once more and Jake's head hit the dash again.

"—me he was—"

Whir-bert crashed Jake's head into the passenger window with a crack.

"I thought he'd be okay." Hailey grabbed at the companion bot but had to return her hand to the wheel to avoid a small family that had run into the road trying to escape the carnage.

Jake took one more blow against the window before he was finally able to grab the little drone and pin it against the dash.

"Don't hurt him!"

"Him?" Jake asked.

"It. Whatever."

Jake opened the glove box and forced the machine inside. He slammed it shut and put his feet up against it.

"I'm sorry, Jake."

Jake nodded and dabbed at his head searching for a sign of blood. "Just get us back to my shop."

Any hope that the carnage was localized dissipated as they made their way across the city. The insanity was happening on every street in the city. News reports were spotty at best as the reporter drones joined the fray and provided only images of the madness they themselves were creating.

The street outside Ashley's Robot Reclamation of Green Hill was no different. Several cars were overturned and burning. Those that weren't sped down the street, careening wildly left and right until they struck enough things to damage the motor. People fled in terror with no idea which direction led to safety. This meant people were constantly running in fear, screaming and doing their best not to get hit by cars.

Jake jumped from the SUV and pounded on the door until Kat

opened it. "Jake. Thank God. Get in here. He's going to kill him."

Jake waved Hailey to pull the truck in and dashed inside. He followed the shouting.

"I'm not a robot! You know that!" It was Glitch and he sounded scared.

"Sounds like something a robot would say." Mason had the big man cornered. He stood behind the massive IMP with the barrel pointed at the cyborg.

"Mason! What are you doing?"

"Just waiting for Rosie here to go revolutionary on us."

"Put it down, you moron," Jake said. "He's not a robot."

"That's what I told him." Glitch didn't move. He had his hands out in front of him as if they would protect him from the devastating pulse.

"Robot arms, robot legs, robot dick. He's a robot all right."

"Think about it, Mason. You know better than anyone that it's a machine's AI that sends it renegade. Glitch doesn't have artificial intelligence. He barely has normal intelligence."

Mason lowered the barrel of the IMP an inch while he considered this. He nodded and backed away. "Yeah, you're right."

Glitch stepped away from the corner. "Thanks, Jake."

Jake put a hand on Glitch's shoulder. "Are you okay?"

"Yeah, he just went nuts all of a sudden."

"I think we both know he's been going nuts for years." He turned back to the shop. "Where the hell is Savant?"

A hand went up behind a bank of computers. "Over here, Jake."

"What?" Jake moved behind the technician. "Why aren't you trying to stop them?"

Savant scanned the screen in front of him. "Oh, I figured it would all work out. I thought a better use of my time would be trying to figure out why the world went berserk."

"What did you find?"

"Oh, nothing. I need a functioning machine to even start looking and everything around here is busted. That's why I suggested we plug in Glitch. That's when Mason went crazy and then you showed up, how are you?"

"Would plugging in Glitch tell us anything?"

"No, Jake. It was a joke, duh. None of you appreciate my humor. I need an AI-driven machine that hasn't been smashed, bashed and shocked into a mess."

Jake ran back to the truck as Hailey stepped out and into the shop. She pointed to Glitch. "What was all that?"

"I hired morons." Jake opened the passenger door and pulled open the glove box. He grabbed at the little bot inside before it could realize what was happening.

Whir-bert struggled against his hold and almost squirmed free once or twice as Jake took him over to Savant. The machine chirped and beeped what Jake could only imagine were unkind words.

"What are you doing to him, Jake?" Hailey asked.

"Don't worry. This won't hurt him." He handed the robot to Savant. "Will this hurt it?"

Savant took the machine and strapped it to a shop table. "No."

"Dammit."

The technician pulled a panel from the back of Whir-bert's head and plugged in a cable before rolling back over to his terminal. The screens began to fill with thousands of lines of code. Savant tapped a few keys and rubbed his chin. "Hmm, interesting."

"What's interesting?" Jake asked.

"Every thing I do, Jake. Every thing I do."

17

The code meant nothing to Jake. He and Hailey peered over Savant's shoulder as the computer scientist scrolled through the gibberish saying things like, "Interesting," "Isn't that something," and "Don't you wish you were as smart as me?"

Jake kicked the technician's chair. "Just tell us what's happening."

"That's just it," Savant said while readjusting his chair. "Nothing is happening."

"Nothing is causing this?"

"No. Something is causing it. Something is flooding the

system with nonsense and garbage code at a ridiculous rate."

"What is the code telling them to do?"

"Nothing, Jake. It's just pure nonsense at an insane speed. Even if it was something, the machines couldn't process it."

"So why the murderous rampage?" Hailey asked.

"It's flooding the system with so much crap that they can't process anything but their most basic programming."

"What about safety protocols?" Jake asked.

"Those are higher level systems. There's so much information coming that they can't even get to that. These things are going to their most base commands. For example, cars go until they stop." He tapped the tiny bot on the table. "Whir-bert here was just trying to cuddle."

"He's a little rough for me," Jake said, touching the wound on his head.

"And it's everything?" Hailey asked. "All systems are being affected?"

Savant shook his head and picked up a remote. He turned on the screen. "Not everything."

Coverage of the devastation was on every channel. Reporters fired line after line of dialogue, hoping that some phrase they uttered would live for eternity next to "Oh, the humanity" as footage of the city in chaos played behind them.

The team watched in silence as the city tore itself apart, hunting through the images for any system that remained immune to the code's effects.

"I'm not seeing it, Savant," Jake said. "Everything looks affected."

"Just watch the news, Jake." The way he said it sounded like a lecture.

"I'm watching the news, Savant."

"Exactly. Duh."

Jake put his face in his hand. The headache was coming back.

Hailey leaned in close to the technician. "Spell it out for us, you complete ass."

Savant sighed a deep breath of attitude. "You're watching the news. The news is reporting it all. The news is showing you footage from their aerial cameras. Which are drones. Which are robots. Which are doing exactly what they are being told to do."

"They aren't being affected," Hailey said.

"I always said she was too smart for you, Jake," Savant said as he idly clicked through the news coverage.

"Wait," Jake reached for the remote. "Go back a channel."

Meagan's face filled the large screen, "—exactly what we feared would happen."

Beneath her image was her name and title: Founder and Director of the Society for the Preservation for Humanity. The reporter spoke to her through the drone. "What do you think is happening?"

"The machines are revolting. History has proven that throughout time any abused population will eventually throw off the yoke of its oppressors and rise up against them. What we are witnessing was inevitable."

"Son of a bitch," Jake muttered.

"The revolution will be televised," Hailey said.

"There is no stopping them now," Meagan continued. "The

best we can hope for is to get through this with minimal loss of life and start passing some common sense robotic laws to prevent this from ever happening again."

Meagan's image reduced down to half the screen when the camera cut back to the anchor at the studio. "Ms. Mouret, you've suffered your fair share of critics and decriers over the years. Many have thought your ideas were pessimistic at best while others called you bat-shit insane. Do you feel today's events have vindicated you? Are you happy to see this happening?"

There was the briefest of smiles before Meagan spoke. "Of course I'm not happy. I pray this comes to a peaceful end quickly before anyone else gets hurt."

"I'm sure we all feel the same. Thank you for your time, Ms. Mouret."

Meagan nodded with a smile as the drone pulled away to a wide shot of a city street. The chaos continued and the anchors did their best to cover the possible reasons for it all. Speculation ranged from ghosts in the machines to gremlins to a terrorist attack.

"Holy shit." Jake pointed at the ZUMR building in the background.

"How did she get down there?" Hailey asked.

"We've got to get down there, too."

"Why?" Mason asked. "Here's perfectly safe. What good will going down there do?"

"Because." Jake snapped his fingers and pointed at Savant.

Savant looked back at the code scrolling across the screen and nodded. "The signal is coming from ZUMR."

"How?" Hailey asked.

"Colton."

The realization dawned on Hailey as the pieces fell together. Her eyes sank to the floor and she shook her head. "That bastard."

Jake rubbed his hands together. "Actually, I'm kind of glad he ended up being the bad guy because now we get to beat the hell out of him. It's not often everything works out the way you hope."

"What do we do, boss?" Glitch asked.

"Load up the Beast," Jake called to the team.

"It's full of holes," Kat said.

Jake turned to the cyborg. "Glitch."

"Yes, Jake?"

"Rip a hole in the roof."

"How big?"

"Big enough for you to sit in. Everyone else grab every piece of gear that still works and put on some montage music. We're building a tank."

With everything jacked up as it was, the only music they could find to play was a thirteenth-century French vocal piece that was stuck in Glitch's RAM. He had to hum it. It was terrible montage music.

Despite this, the team worked quickly. Ratchets cranked and torches arced in a flurry of sparks.

Glitch tore a Glitch-sized hole in the Beast's roof and mounted the IMP on an articulated armature Jake welded together from several junked machines.

Kat layered the trucks with wire and connected the structure to several generators.

Savant set to gutting inoperable equipment and cobbling together functional weapons.

Mason complained a lot about how much work he was doing compared to what he thought the others were doing.

Despite the speed at which they worked, everything went smoothly. The only exception being when Hailey had to stretch across the hood of the truck to reach a tool and her ankle showed. Glitch lost his focus and dragged a welding torch across his hand, fusing his index, middle and ring fingers together.

The cyborg held up his hand. "Aw, man. Not again."

Savant heard the moaning. "What's wrong, Glitch?"

The cyborg held up the mangled appendage. "Now I've got to wear my old hand. It's so ugly."

"I used it for parts."

"You what?!"

"It's not like you were using it. It was just sitting there forever."

"Now what am I going to do? I can't fight in a robot Armageddon with just one hand."

"Not so fast, Sad Sack of Parts." Savant turned back to his shop table and picked up the project he had been working on. It was hardly gleaming with chrome, and it actually was still smoking in places but it was a pair of hands. A giant pair of hands.

"My old hands!"

"No. Your new old hands," Savant said. He walked over to Glitch and helped the giant put his new hands on. "Twice the size and five times the grip strength. You should be able to crush any bot like it was nothing. Don't try and pee with them though."

Glitch held up his massive new hands and flexed each finger before tightening each into a coconut-sized fist. He said nothing to Savant. He only smiled.

Jake opened the gun vault in his office and began handing Hailey several shotguns which she laid out on the desk. He handed her a revolver in a holster and a box of ammo. "This one's for you. Please don't get killed out there."

"Oh, that's so sweet," she said with little sincerity. "I kind of figured you'd tell me to wait here where it's safe."

"I was going to, but we don't have time to go through the whole argument where you convince me I'm being controlling et cetera and so forth.

"So just know that I feel shame and take the gun. And try not to die out there because I really like being around you. Still."

"You know me so well." Hailey took the gun and tucked the holster into her waistline. "I'd also like you not to die out there. Okay?"

Jake took her hands and looked into her eyes. "Because you really like being around me?"

Her smile went crooked and she lowered her voice. "Because I'm pretty sure I'm going to need a new job after all this is done."

"You're hired," he leaned in closer. "No one here has been paid in weeks. What's one more on the payroll?"

Hailey leaned in, too. Their lips were less than an inch apart.

"Oh, please don't ask about the perks," Savant said from the doorway.

"Savant!" Jake shouted.

"It would be so expected. She asks about the perks, you say

'let me show you' and then you sweep the shotguns off the desk and go at it. I've seen it a hundred times, okay. It's just so cliché."

"Did you find him?" Mason shouted from the shop floor.

"Yeah," Savant yelled back out the door. "He's in here being gross with his ex."

"She's not my ex," Jake said and started looking for the aspirin. "What do you want, Savant?"

"We're ready to go out here. You wanna go save the city or should it wait for you two to do your thing?"

"Get out."

Savant backed out of the office and shut the door while Hailey scooped up the shotguns in her arms.

Jake turned back to Hailey and smiled. "Where were we?"

"You were about to go save the city and I was going to go report this incident to HR."

"I should never have hired you."

"It's too late now." She dropped the shotguns into Jake's arms. "Let's go beat the hell out of Colton."

18

The door rolled and the sound of the chaos rushed in.

Sirens, alarms and screaming filled the night as panic washed over the city. The smell of a thousand fires wafted into the garage and stung their eyes. The city services were on the grid. Everything was on the grid. And the grid wasn't working.

Traffic still filled the streets and the self-piloted cars sped by at full throttle with terrified passengers glued to the windows praying for the batteries to run dry.

Night had fallen and the city lights weren't helping with the darkness. They flashed in seizure-inducing sequences, switching from one color to the next with no apparent pattern. They painted the streets in a rainbow strobe that made everything appear jerky.

Kat fed the Beast four barrels full of fuel and the truck lurched out onto the street. Glitch bounced in the hole behind the IMP while Savant slid back and forth across the bench seat manning the passenger windows.

Hailey gunned the black SUV into the road behind them with Jake and Mason each covering a window in the rear.

The ride hadn't improved since Hailey and Jake had arrived earlier. The streets were in complete chaos and the cars were piling up as they plowed into already substantial wrecks that lined the roads.

A cab shot across the road in front of the Beast, forcing Kat to stomp on the brakes. Hailey swerved to the right and came alongside the red SUV. The two trucks rode side by side down the road.

"You want me to start shooting now, Jake?" Glitch asked over the radio from the top of the Beast.

"Only if someone's in danger. Don't draw their attention. If they're content to ignore us, let's keep it that way."

Savant scoffed. "I told you idiots already, they're just being overwhelmed to the point of confusion. They're following their base programming. They are not, I repeat, they are not being directed."

"Good. Let's hope it stays that way."

"Of course it's going to stay that way. It's been that way for hours and it probably took quite a lot to pull this off. Why would it change now? Think, Jake. You never think."

Jake dropped the mic and just shook his head.

"Why do you keep him around?" Hailey asked.

"Because—as much as it sucks—he's always right."

The radio snapped on again and Savant sighed. "Hey, Jake?"

"What is it, Savant?"

"The code just changed. They, uh, they're being directed now."

"What?!"

"But they weren't before and I want to be clear on that."

A HomeBot 4000 Domestic Assistant charged across the street and leapt onto the black SUV's running board.

Jake grabbed the handle to roll down the window just as the machine ripped the door off and threw it into the street.

He pulled the trigger on his disruptor and the robot shook as the current enveloped it and shut down its systems. Jake kicked the dead machine from the side of the truck as traffic started steering toward them.

"Kat!" he yelled into the mic. "Get in front of us and have Glitch start clearing a path. Don't hurt anyone."

The Beast cut back in front of the SUV. The bloop of the IMP was inaudible to Jake over the sound of the engines and wind rushing by his open door, but the effect was obvious. Vehicles that had swung toward them fizzed and popped as the massive EMP blast ripped through their motors and melted their hoods.

Glitch whooped as he pulled the trigger over and over again. "I don't know what Mason did to this, but it is hot!"

The street was no longer filled with random vehicles and machines. It was now flooding with cars and bots from across the city. And they were all heading straight for the team.

Glitch's IMP took out cars as fast as he could pull the trigger and the women behind the wheels avoided the rest, but the smaller machines were getting through.

Jake, Mason and Savant fired out the windows as the machines rushed from apartments and storefronts. BettyCrockerbots ran from the bakeries swinging rolling pins. LawnBots chased after them with hedge clippers. Mary Bottins ran down the street flinging soiled diapers that thwacked against the car in disgusting smears that the windshield wipers were powerless against.

The cobbled-together disruptors held as the team fired at each of the attackers. A Grease Monkey XJ dropped its wrenches and clattered to the ground in a blast of blue current, while its supervisor fell a moment later as Mason unloaded on the AutoBot.

Working together, the teams kept the threat at bay with little more than a few bumps and bangs from the larger traffic on the road. This all changed when they passed the massage parlor.

Rub-It-Out Massage Parlor's front window exploded and two dozen Masseusenators dashed toward them blaring, "Tell us where you're tense." The men fired repeatedly and managed to stop several, but there were too many.

The Masseusenators crawled over the SUVs, their pneumatic hands pounding against metal. The Beast held but Hailey's SUV was soon rattling from loose body panels.

One of the bots crawled on top of Glitch and began pounding the giant in the back. The cyborg screamed and grabbed the slender robot in his big hands. With one squeeze he crushed its head and tossed it onto the road.

"There're too many of them," Hailey yelled as the windshield cracked in a massive spider web. "I can't see."

The radio squawked as Savant yelled into the mic. "Activate the Savant cage."

Mason reached over the back seat and grabbed the makeshift switch. "That's what we're calling it?"

"Does it matter?" Jake pulled the disruptor trigger as a Masseusenator reached into the cab. The disruptor sizzled and smoked but did not discharge.

"I refuse to call it that."

"Just hit it!"

Mason flipped the switch and the SUV was instantly enveloped in the smell of ozone and sparks. The generators pumped their current through the wire cage affixed to the SUV's exterior and through the Masseusenators.

The parlor bots collapsed to the top of the truck and rolled into the street to be crushed beneath the truck's wheels.

The Beast sparked a moment later with the same result and dropped another five machines beneath Hailey's wheels.

They were getting close when a fire truck's lights lit up the street in front of them. Red strobes flooded their windshields as the service vehicle sped toward them with the sirens blaring. The massive hook and ladder turned sharply across the street and drove through a glass storefront, while the bot on the back cranked the wheel and brought the rear of the truck up onto the opposite sidewalk blocking the entire street.

Hailey and Kat slammed on the brakes that didn't work so

well.

Several F1RST brand SafetyMan 100s stepped from the engine. The powerful machines were built thick. Their servos were strong enough to lift girders. Their skeletons were durable enough to survive a structural collapse. And their skin was built to withstand the most intense heat and shielded from electrical charges.

They came with axes. They came with hoses. One moved toward them with the Jaws of Life chomping at a rate never intended by the manufacturer. Their faces flashed in sync with the emergency lights on the truck as they painted the darkened street a horrifying red.

The bloop of the IMP sounded with no meaningful response. It did knock the helmet from one machine, but that wasn't enough to stop it. It didn't even go back for the hat.

It was heartbreaking to see such an iconic and heroic figure moving toward them in such a menacing manner. Firefighters had been heroes since childhood. Everyone's childhood. It caused Jake to hesitate.

The Beast's backup lights popped on and the truck shot into reverse.

One of the machines dashed around the red goliath and stood behind it.

Kat slammed into the machine.

It hardly moved an inch. The SafetyMan's feet were dug into the asphalt and its hands were braced against the Beast's rear.

The Travelall's tire began to spin and smoke. It wasn't going anywhere.

Jake grabbed a shotgun and jumped through the hole where his door used to be. He pumped a slug into the chamber. He pulled the stock to his shoulder and swung the barrel toward the SafetyMan 100 behind the Beast.

The first shot knocked the helmet from the machine's head. He pumped another slug into the shotgun. The second shot went straight into the air as Jake jumped backward. He caught motion out of the corner of his eye and stepped away just as the ax spun past his face and embedded itself in the SUV's hood.

Jake turned to fire at the ax-throwing first responder.

It was too close. It charged through the street and was almost upon him when it jerked back and the report from Mason's shotgun sounded.

The SafetyMan reacquired its target quickly and charged once more.

This time a slug caught it in the side as Kat stepped from the Beast with a smoking gun.

The SafetyMan recovered from Kat's shot and stood. Hailey's finished it off.

Glitch dropped from the roof and grabbed another machine by the throat in mid-stride as it ran to join the fight. He slammed it against the ground until it stopped moving.

The rest of the engine's members turned their attention away from the vehicles and focused on the humans that were dumb enough to get out of their cars.

Jake and his team gathered in the middle of the street and frantically reloaded. All except for the computer scientist.

Jake pulled the stock to his shoulder and yelled toward the

Beast, "Savant! You want to help us out here?"

"I'm helping just fine from in here thank you."

"We could really use your help out here!"

"You need it in here more."

"I think I know better than you what I need!"

"Yeah, you'd think so."

Kat pumped a shell into her gun. "I really hate him, Jake. So much."

"And you're right to hate him, Kat."

The SafetyMen charged and the team opened up. Shotgun blasts filled the canyon-like street with a thunderous chaos that reigned over the truck's sirens.

The team pumped slug after slug into the oncoming machines but the firebots did not fall easy. It took seven shots to stop one and though it fell to the ground, the Jaws of Life chomped on.

They were driving another one back when the water started. The blast knocked Hailey from her feet and threw Mason back against the SUV's hood.

The fire team turned the hose on Kat and she braced herself for the force.

Glitch screamed and jumped in front of the mechanic. His massive chest took the blast of water as he planted his feet.

The firefighters turned up the pressure and Glitch began to struggle with his footing. He growled against the water and found his traction once more. He screamed at the machines, "You leave her alone!"

Piston driven steps propelled the cyborg forward against the insane pressure from the hose. The stream burst across his chest and soaked the streets until water ran into the storm sewers.

The pressure increased once more as a second SafetyMan helped brace the hose as Glitch slowed. But he did not stop. He reached the end of the hose and placed one of his giant hands over the nozzle.

The water stopped.

He reached out with the other hand and grabbed the firebot by the face. He threw the machine aside and let go of the nozzle. It shot away from his palm like a bullet, carrying the other SafetyMan with it back over the truck.

Kat screamed for Glitch as the rest of the team was overrun.

The shotgun blasts were less frequent now as they tried to reload between shots.

The firefighter squad came at them with axes and bare hands that were no less lethal.

An ax came for Jake's head and he raised the shotgun to block it. He stopped the blade from cleaving his head open but the swing drove him to the ground. The machines were just too strong.

The SafetyMan pulled back to swing again.

Jake dropped the shotgun and drew his pistol. He placed three shots in the machine's face and it did nothing to stop it.

Hailey screamed as a machine grabbed her. Kat swore as she was knocked to the ground. Glitch screamed and raced back to the group and the firebot swung the ax again.

It stopped inches from his head.

Hailey stopped screaming. Kat kept swearing but with far less fear and much more anger. Glitch arrived in the center of it all.

He shoved one of the frozen machines and watched it topple to the ground. "What the hell happened?"

"I happened!" Savant stood in the turret of the Beast and gloated. "I told you that you wanted me in there."

Jake pushed over another one of the machines. "What did you do?"

"Ha. I haven't done anything yet." Savant ducked back into the Beast to his workstation.

The SafetyMen sprang back to life but they did not attack. They backed away from the team with no threatening moves and gathered their dropped equipment. They then lined up shoulder-to-shoulder and saluted.

"Haha!" Savant was back on the roof.

"What is this?" Kat asked.

Savant was unbearable when he had no reason to gloat. Now he had a reason. "My code-fu is better than their code-fu."

The fire truck cut its emergency light and silenced the siren. There was a crash of debris and falling glass as the hook and ladder truck backed out of the storefront. It straightened out with the engine pointing toward ZUMR headquarters. The SafetyMen jumped on the truck and settled in until ready to respond at their next destination.

"We've now got an escort," Savant said. "Thanks to me. I just want to make that clear."

19

The convoy continued to grow.

Whatever Savant had done—everyone wondered but no one cared enough to listen to the explanation—was having a pacifying effect on every machine they encountered.

Cars still swerved toward them and the machines still charged at them, but once they got close enough their aggressive nature disappeared. The machines simply turned to follow the Beast and the black SUV behind the massive fire truck.

By the time they reached ZUMR, more than two hundred and fifty cars and their passengers surrounded them.

"Savant, are you sure its safe to get out?" Jake asked over the radio.

"Duh," Savant scolded over the radio.

Jake stepped out of the SUV. The cars made no move to charge. The machines that had followed made no move to attack. He turned slowly and saw the passengers looking back at him with questions on their faces and fear in their eyes.

The rest of the team joined him.

"This is eerie," Hailey said as she looked at the idle machines surrounding them.

Glitch waved an arm at the assembled robots. There was no response. "They're all just sitting there."

"This is weird," Kat said.

"I don't like it," Jake agreed.

"Glitch smells," said Mason.

"I do not. Shut up, Mason."

"Enough," Jake silenced them. "As much as it pains us, we have to trust whatever Savant did."

"Uh," Savant's voice filled the radio. "What I did was single handedly quell a robot uprising all by myself."

Jake shook his head. "Fine. Next we need a plan to get Porter out of there. He's going to be bunkered in. And he's losing control, so he's going to be desperate. There's no telling how he may act."

The doors to the ZUMR tower crashed open and Colton Porter came running down the stairs toward them. "Hailey. Oh, thank God you're here."

"This is a weird trick," Kat muttered to Jake.

Colton ran wildly toward Hailey with outstretched arms.

Glitch stepped in front of her and stuck out one of his giant, new hands.

The momentum Colton had built and the force of the punch sent him flipping to the ground.

"That's for making my junk famous," Glitch said.

Jake pulled the cyborg back and shouted at Colton. "Get up. Because I owe you one for the video, too." Colton spit a mouth full of blood onto the street. "I didn't do this! This isn't me!"

"Yeah, right."

"It wasn't me!" Porter looked to Hailey for help. There was none coming from her.

Hailey made a fist of her own. "The signal is coming from here, Colton. We know you sent out the code to overwhelm the machines. We know when you started directing them to attack us. If it wasn't for Savant, they'd still be after us."

Savant stuck his head through the hole in the Beast's roof. "That's right."

"No." Porter sounded scared. He looked scared. "That... that wasn't you. It changed from here."

"Hardly," Savant snorted.

Jake ignored him and kept his focus on Porter. "So you admit it? That's a new level of stupid, even for you."

"No, it wasn't me, it..."

The front of the ZUMR building exploded into a rain of fire and glass.

The SafetyMan fire team sprang into action. The first truck jumped the curb and pulled onto the pavilion in front of the building. The machines dismounted and set to work with their hoses.

The towering flames faded quickly, and through the smoke and rising steam Jake and Hailey spotted the cause of the explosion at the same time.

"Project Cupcake," they said together as the walking tank strode forward and kicked the fire truck to the curb.

More glass shattered and the steel window frames snapped as the military giant stepped out of ZUMR headquarters and into the street. The walking tank stood motionless for only a second before the guns on its arms starting spinning up.

"Spinny-gun!" Glitch shouted and ran back to the Beast.

"Everyone duck!" Jake grabbed Hailey and pulled her behind the Beast.

The team scattered as the guns blazed to life.

Chunks of asphalt leapt from the street as bullets buried themselves in the ground. They weren't even close to where the team was standing. Project Cupcake shifted its feet as it attempted to fine tune its aim.

"It looks like it's still working on its targeting," Jake said from behind the relative safety of the Beast. Judging from the state the street was in, even the Travelall's solid steel mass wouldn't protect them.

"That bastard lied to me," Hailey said. "He said it wasn't operational."

"He told us both that having the CPU in the same building was a violation of the treaties." Jake shrugged. "But, he lied about a lot of things. This really shouldn't surprise us."

Project Cupcake found its footing and aimed dead center at the

Beast.

Mason shouted, "Hit it, Glitch!"

Glitch pulled the IMP from the roof of the Beast and fired.

The bloop sounded and kicked and for a moment nothing happened.

A panel popped open on the machine's shoulder and a rocket shot into the air.

The team watched the brilliant arc paint the sky and lost the projectile behind a building. Ten seconds later they heard an explosion.

Glitch lowered the IMP's barrel. "That wasn't me."

"It's shielded, you moron." Porter was as low to the ground as a snake could get. "Shooting it's not going to do anything."

Mason pulled a shotgun to his chest. "How do you propose we stop it then?"

Porter shook his head. "You can't. It's bulletproof, fireproof, impervious to EMPs, electric shock, missiles and anything else you might use to stop a giant fucking tank."

Project Cupcake moved into the street with earthshaking steps.

Trapped inside, passengers beat against their car windows looking for escape. Jake could see the terror in their eyes and imagined that more than a few of the vehicles were starting to stink.

"Savant." Jake pointed at the dead cars around them. "Can you get these people out of here?"

Savant was curled up next to the tire, pounding frantically on his tablet. "I can't. Something is fighting me on this."

The news drones had begun to gather on the square. They

hovered around the military machine, lighting its various weapon systems with their spotlights.

Hailey pointed to the floating cameras. "Whoever is doing this, they still want it televised."

"Savant, can you get control of the news cameras?"

His fingers moved at impossible speeds across the tablet. "Um, no. I can't."

"Why not?"

"Look, I'm not really sure how to tell you this—especially after all the gloating I did." It was the first time Savant had ever sounded unsure of his words. "But, I don't think I'm doing any of this."

"What do you mean?"

The arrogance returned with a contempt-filled sigh. "I'm saying, I think this asshole is right." He jerked a thumb toward Colton.

Everything around them sprang to life. The cars lurched in all directions. They began running into one another in longer and faster bursts as they cleared room around the Beast.

The robots that had managed to keep up with the convoy began to march toward the team taking shelter behind the Travelall. More began to fill the streets and move toward the place in front of the building.

Several more rockets launched from Project Cupcake and rained down on different parts of the city.

Jake looked at the approaching army of machines as the Beast bucked against them with each collision. "Everybody inside!"

"You're crazy!" Porter screamed as the rest of the team got to their feet.

They rushed through the plaza as the machines came at them. Glitch cleared a path with the IMP as the rest of the team held back the mechanical forces with everything they had left.

The walking tank chased after them with a stream of bullets fired from the mini-guns on its arms. Its aim had improved slightly and the stone tile shattered beneath their feet.

They cleared the lobby and the bullets chased them inside. The displays left uncrushed by Project Cupcake's dramatic entrance were now destroyed by its guns. Glass display cases exploded. Displays sparked. And the prototypes on display were shredded as the team raced to the stairway.

Glitch ripped the handrail from the wall and twisted it into something resembling a lock for the door. Moments later, the fire door began to shudder as the army of robots crashed into it.

Once inside, Jake took a head count. Everyone had made it. Even Porter.

"I thought you weren't coming," Kat said.

"I wasn't going to stay out there. That bitch is crazy."

"What bitch?" Jake asked.

He pointed to the door. "Cupcake."

Jake grabbed him by the shoulder and slammed him against the wall. "Who is behind this?"

"No one. It's the uprising."

Hailey pulled Jake away and smashed Colton across the face with her shotgun, sending him to the ground.

"Hey," Jake said. "Would everyone please stop punching this asshole before I can?"

"There's a line!" She turned her attention to Colton. "Tell me."

Porter closed his eyes and spoke. "It's that humans first chick. She's behind this."

"Meagan?" Jake asked and received a nod. "How? How did she get access? You?"

Porter shrugged.

"Unbelievable." Hailey kicked him in the ribs. "Why?"

Porter shrugged again. "Money. She's loaded."

"And let me guess," Jake interrupted. "She promised no one would get hurt."

"We never really talked about that."

Hailey kicked him again.

"Why does Hailey keep kicking him?" Mason asked. "I think it's only fair that we all get a kick."

"All I did was give her access to the signal. Okay? She's the one doing all the violence."

Hailey kicked him once more. "Where?"

Mason threw up his arms. "There she goes again. Jake, are you going to do something about this or do I need to call my union rep?"

Porter sputtered something that Hailey understood. She kicked him once more and said, "Follow me."

The team followed her up the stairs, with only Mason hanging back to give Porter one more kick.

20

Somewhere around the 3rd floor they heard Glitch's lock fail.

The party stopped in mid-stride and from below they could hear the sound of a hundred metallic feet charging up the stairs.

"We're almost there," Hailey said as she charged on.

"Thank God," Glitch said as he started back up the stairs.

"Oh, up yours, robot legs." Mason pushed past him. "You don't get to bitch."

Once on the fifth floor, the team piled everything they could find against the fire door and followed Hailey down the hallway.

She led them to a command center and Jake held the door

open as the team filed in. Down the hall he could see the pile against the door shake as the army pounded against it. It appeared to be holding.

Jake stepped into the ZUMR command center. A hundred monitors lined the consoles. Each one showed streams of erratic code running at impossible speeds. "Savant, get on it."

Without a word the computer scientist jumped into a chair and began analyzing the feed.

"Uh, Jake." Glitch stood by the window. The night sky flashed with explosions behind him.

"What is it, Glitch?" He stepped around Kat and Mason and joined the giant at the window. "Oh. Well, shit."

The plaza was full of machines of every make and model, and those that could were scaling the side of the building.

"Savant?"

"I'm being amazing as fast as I can, Jake."

Kat stood by the door and shouted, "Jake!"

He rushed across the room and saw the problem. The office drones were at the fire door and they were removing the barricade.

He opened the door and the two began to fire.

The fifth-floor bathroom attendant fell before the machines realized what was happening. Half of the machines turned their attention to the command center as the rest continued to break down the barricade.

Jake called for Mason to join them as the machines charged.

Voltage and lead filled the hallway as the three of them held back the onslaught of office bots. Coffee drones dropped to the ground. Kitchen monitors exploded with a final desperate plea to clean out the fridge. But as the pile of scrap built in front of them, the pile against the door was cleared away.

The stairwell door smashed in, crushing a paper shredder between it and the wall, as an army of robots spilled into the hall.

"Savant?!"

"Almost there. Geez."

"Savant, you'd better hurry," Glitch called as he backed away from the window.

Savant grunted and hung his head between his shoulders. "Okay. I need an antenna." He stood and yanked a cord from the back of the computer console. "Glitch, come here."

The cyborg happily stepped farther from the window.

"Take this cable."

Glitch grabbed the cable. He yipped and pulled his hand back. "It shocked me."

"It's going to, but I need you to be my antenna."

"Just do it, Glitch!" Mason screamed. "They're everywhere out here."

Glitch grit his teeth against the pain and took the wire.

"Now I need you to go over to the window."

The window cracked as the first machine reached the floor and smashed its way into the room.

Glitch grabbed it by the head as it charged across the room and crushed its skull. "I don't want to go to the window."

"Glitch, you've got to get to that window!" Savant was back at the keyboard frantically pounding in commands.

Several more machines broke through from outside the building and stormed into the room.

Jake and Hailey turned their shotguns against them but Glitch was soon overwhelmed as he made his way to the edge of the floor.

It was only his willpower and cyborg legs that carried him the last few feet as more machines piled on top of him. "It's not working!"

Savant screamed over his shoulder. "You have to beep!"

"What?!"

"Beep. Like an antenna."

"Antennas don't beep." Glitch winced as one of the surviving Masseusenators began pounding on his back.

"Yes they do, you just can't hear them like a robot can."

Mason and Kat ran into the room and slammed the door. "There're too many."

The crash against the door shook the entire room.

"Beep, damn you!"

"Beep, beep, beep, beep."

The chaos ended. The machines stopped attacking. They backed away from the team and stood waiting for a command as if nothing had happened.

"Yes!" Savant leapt from the chair with his arms in the air. "My code-fu is…"

"Can I let go of this now?" Glitch had developed a twitch in his face from the current.

"Yeah, that wasn't doing anything anyway."

"What?! Then why?"

"Because you were rushing me. I don't like being rushed."

"And the beeping?"

"I thought it was hilarious."

Glitch threw down the cable and stomped toward Savant.

Jake stepped in between them. "Savant, is it over?"

"Yes, it's over Jake. I shut down her signal and saved the day. Again. All you have to do now is find her and turn her crazy ass in. And I'm out on that by the way. I'm a little tired now and I'd like to go to bed."

"Guys." Mason stood at the window looking out to the street below. "That tank is still moving. And, I'm not sure how, but it looks pissed."

Savant turned back to his screen and started typing furiously. "That's not possible. Everything with an AI should be running through here."

"It's not an AI," Glitch said as he stared at the machine. He looked into the room and several monitors changed to show his perspective on the screens. Glitch looked back at the machine. He focused on the cockpit and zoomed in.

Through the thick glass in its torso, the team stared at the screen as Glitch's visions flicked through several different filters until one revealed Meagan behind the controls.

"They never installed the processor. Jack wasn't lying."

"Yeah," Jake agreed. "But remember he lied about a lot of other things."

Mason pointed at the screen. "It's Jake's uncle's girlfriend!"

"She's driving that thing?" Mason asked. "No wonder it couldn't shoot."

Project Cupcake let loose another salvo of rockets.

Jake rushed to the window. "It looks like she's getting better.

We have to stop her."

Savant folded his arms across his chest and leaned back in the chair. "Sure, let me just grab my tank."

Jake waved his hand around the room at the docile machines. "Can you control these things?"

"I can do anything."

"Kiss a girl?" Kat asked.

Savant blushed. "I haven't met the right one yet."

Jake raced across the room and opened the door. The hallway was filled with hundreds of robots awaiting a purpose. "I need a real answer here, Savant."

"Yes, I can do it."

Jake motioned for Kat to turn around. The look on her face said she didn't understand, but she turned and Jake removed her disruptor pack. He crossed the room and held out the pack to Glitch.

The cyborg took the pack in his hands. "What's this for?"

Jake smiled. "We're going to get her attention."

"Jake, are you sure about this?" Hailey asked.

Mason raised his hand. "I'm with her. This sounds like a terrible idea."

Jake ignored their comments and spoke firmly to Glitch. "When I say, you throw that thing at her. Do you understand?"

"Yeah, Jake, I understand but I'm kind of with these guys on this one. If she doesn't know we're here I don't think we should tell her."

"Just get ready." Jake picked up his shotgun and loaded several fresh slugs. "Everyone else against the wall. Not you,

Savant. Stay on the keys."

Glitch moved closer to the edge of the window while politely asking several of the robots to clear a space.

Jake pushed in the last shell and pumped the gun. He stood next to Glitch for a moment before tucking the stock into his shoulder. "Now."

Glitch reared back and heaved the disruptor pack into the darkness. The heavy pack arced through the air and began its descent as it neared Project Cupcake.

Jake followed its path with the shotgun and pulled the trigger.

In the distance, the pack exploded with a blinding blue ring of electricity as it passed in front of Project Cupcake's cockpit, causing the machine to stumble and slowly turn.

"I think it worked," Glitch said.

"Dammit," Mason said as he moved closer to the wall.

"Get ready, Savant." Jake watched the walking tank turn toward them. "That's right. Come over here. Come on over."

"Jake, stop talking to it."

The massive machine stepped toward the building and raised its arms.

"Spinny-gun," Glitch said, and tackled Jake out of the way as bullets riddled the room.

Savant dove behind a console and yelled, "Well, she's learned how to aim. What's the rest of your plan?"

"Let her get a little closer."

"Are you insane?" Kat screamed.

The building began to shake as Meagan stomped closer. Lead and glass flew around the room. Seats were shredded into plastic and stuffing. The walls turned into powder as the drywall did nothing to slow the rounds. The robots in the room made no attempt to get out of the way and several of them soaked up the bullets until they collapsed.

The shaking was ridiculous and ceiling panels began to drop from above.

The bullets stopped and Jake stood up from behind what little cover there was.

Meagan was just outside the window.

Jake moved to the middle of the room. Circuits popped and sparked around him. Parts of the room were still falling in. He stopped in the middle of it all and raised his arms.

Project Cupcake reached up and put one hand on the edge of the window and pulled itself up to the fifth floor. The right hand reached into the window and opened its fingers, reaching for Jake.

He stepped out of the fingers' reach and swept both hands toward Meagan's mech. "Send them all!"

Savant shot up in his seat, realizing this was his cue. His fingers slapped against the keyboard in rapid strokes and the dormant army of robots sprang to life once more.

Every machine that filled the halls and hung from the side of the ZUMR building, every robot in the plaza and the streets below swarmed over Project Cupcake.

Those that were close climbed onto the mech's arm and scrambled toward its body.

The giant hand tried to shake the machines free and shook the building with each swing. But the robots held fast and soon Meagan backed away into the street.

Jake stood motionless, knowing the flood of machines would flow around him as they rushed to the edge of the window and leapt into the air. Most landed with a clang somewhere on Project Cupcake's body. Those that missed were replaced by others as machines continued to arrive from around the city.

The mech began to stumble and flail as it tried to brush the robots away, but the legion covered it from head to toe and began to pull it apart.

The swarm ejected pieces of the machine as it began to strip away the outer shell.

Guns fired and rockets launched as Meagan did everything she could to stop the swarm. But soon the weapons fell silent as the robot mass worked its way to those systems as well.

A minute later they got to the knee and Project Cupcake collapsed in the ZUMR plaza. More machines piled on and continued to tear away. It wasn't long before the massive machine wasn't even visible from the command center. But the news drones were seeing everything.

Jake pulled out his phone and found the news feed. He put the projection up in the room and the team watched as the robots stripped away the cockpit and revealed Meagan Mouret to the viewing public.

She screamed and continued to throttle the now unresponsive controls.

"Call them off, Savant." Jake smiled as the cameras got their close up.

The machines stopped their assault and began to back away, leaving Meagan alone with her new infamy.

21

By the time they reached the bottom floor, a team of SafetyMen were cutting Meagan from the cockpit while the authorities stood by waiting to take her into custody.

Robot medics tended to the trapped passengers, and city service machines began to clean up the debris and shell casings that filled the streets.

The news drones hovered around the rescue operation capturing B-roll footage while waiting for the big arrest.

It wasn't long before the cameras began peeling off from the wreckage and headed their way.

"Ready for your close-up?" Hailey smiled and nodded toward the cameras.

"Absolutely not. I've had enough cameras in my face to last me quite a while."

"Don't worry, boss." Savant stepped toward the oncoming drones. "I'll talk to them."

"No, you won't." Jake looked at Kat. "Would you please handle this?"

"I'm just the mechanic."

"You're also the only articulate one here. Just tell them what happened and don't let Savant or Mason say anything."

"Okay."

"And don't let Glitch talk about his junk."

"Okay."

"Or ankles. Don't let him talk about ankles."

"Of course not."

"And make sure to give our phone number."

"You sure you don't want to handle this, Jake?" Kat asked.

"No. I'm sorry. You'll do fine."

The team members stepped into the light of the cameras and were soon engulfed by the drones.

"It's one hell of a team you've got, Jake," Hailey said.

"It's a great team. You still want that job?"

Hailey rolled her eyes.

"It pays shit. And I mean like nothing."

She put her arms around him.

"And the first month's paycheck is probably going to be late. I'm going to need it to find a place to live."

They kissed and he didn't think about it. It wasn't weird anymore. It was wonderful. There were no other people or other problems to worry about. He enjoyed every moment of it until a drone buzzed past his head and broke their embrace.

Several more zipped by, speeding toward the ZUMR building as another figure emerged from the shattered lobby.

Colton had somehow escaped the onslaught of machines and stood on the plaza steps calling for the news crew.

"He's going to stand there and just lie his ass off."

"Maybe not. I've got a plan." Jake took Hailey's hand and together they ran up the steps toward him.

Porter was directing the drones. Telling them which side was his good side.

Hailey ran up to him. "Colton? How did you... you're okay!"

"No thanks to you or your friends." He said "friends" with a glare in Jake's direction.

Jake shrugged. "I'm glad you're okay, Porter."

"No, you're—"

It was the most satisfying punch Jake had ever thrown. The force was just right. The sound was perfect. He connected with every knuckle and every ounce of anger all at once and Colton Porter went down hard during a live broadcast.

"Oh, I like this plan," Hailey said.

Porter's lip was swollen before his ass hit the ground. He tried to swear but teeth fell out through the words. He could talk to the reporters all he wanted but they wouldn't understand a word of it, and since the public was too lazy to read subtitles, Kat would have a chance to tell the truth before the rumors started.

Jake looked at the man on the ground. "Colton, you have my permission to post that video anywhere you like."

He turned and offered Hailey his arm. "If you don't mind, I'd love to escort you back to your place and your bed. Where I will instantly fall asleep and not wake up for several days."

"How can I say no to that?"

THE END

* * * *

Read Benjamin Wallace's bestselling post-apocalyptic comedies, the Duck & Cover adventures.

The end of the world as you've never known it.

Post-Apocalyptic Nomadic Warriors (A Duck & Cover Adventure Book 1)
Knights of the Apocalypse (A Duck & Cover Adventure Book 2)
Pursuit of the Apocalypse (A Duck & Cover Adventure Book 3)
Tales of the Apocalypse (Volume 1) - Summer 2016

AVAILABLE ON AMAZON

* * * *

ABOUT THE AUTHOR

Benjamin Wallace lives in Texas where he complains about the heat.

Visit the author at benjaminwallacebooks.com.
Also, find him on twitter @BenMWallace or on facebook.

Or you can email him at: *contact@benjaminwallacebooks.com*

To learn about the latest releases and giveaways, join his Readers' Group at benjaminwallacebooks.com.

If you enjoyed *JUNKERS* please consider leaving a review. It would be very much appreciated and help more than you could know.

Thanks for reading, visiting, following and sharing.
-ben

Printed in Great Britain
by Amazon